Jonelle hef

said, "Everybod

From the ot

chorus of "Yes, Boss" and "Let's go!"

The Lightning's deployment doors opened out over the icy ground strewn with rocks and boulders. It helped a little that the Lightning's jets had blown the site mostly clear of snow, but around the Scout there was still a fair amount, and the wind whipping past them was bringing more in the beginnings of drifts from the upper slopes of the neighboring mountain. At least there was no danger of an avalanche: all the snow that could fall down in the immediate neighborhood had fallen down.

Fire erupted from the downed Scout. It might not be able to fly, but at least some of whatever aliens were inside it were apparently all right. This annoyed Jonelle, and made her suspect that the inmates were of the more robust types of aliens. *Damn.*

X-COM
UFO Defense™

A Novel

X-COM
UFO Defense™

A Novel

by
Diane Duane

Prima Publishing

ISBN: 0-7615-0235-1
Library of Congress Catalog Card Number: 95-074905
Printed in the United States of America

95 96 97 98 EE 10 9 8 7 6 5 4 3 2 1

One

It was dark that night in the streets of Ravenna. Even in the first years of the twenty-first century, the streets didn't have much more light than they had when the place was still the second city of the dying Roman Empire. Too many city councils fond of kickbacks had siphoned off funds from "unnecessary" public lighting budgets again and again, and the crooked contractors had done the rest of the job, leaving the city's narrow streets drowned in a near-premedieval gloom. There were exceptions to the rule, of course—such as tonight, when the place was better lit than usual, not by moonlight, but by muzzle flashes.

The horizontal lightning of energy weapons stitched the dark air, leaving everything stinking of ozone, and all the air so ionized that your hair stood up in it like a cat's fur stroked in dry weather. Sparks jumped from everything that wasn't already singed or on fire, which at the moment wasn't much. The alien craft had landed at one end of the Piazza dei San Vitale, starting what Ari could only assume was intended as a terror mission. They started it very well, by the simple expedient of either frying or crushing to death the several hundred people in the open air there. They had been sitting drinking *espresso corto* or *vino rosso* in the close, airless stillness of an unusually warm autumn night, eating pastas and honey pastries, talking and laughing the night away. Then the night had come down on them in a blaze of thrusters and a crushing weight, and now not much was left of them but their screams, by now mostly faded to sporadic faint moans and weeping. Around the piazza, everything was dark now, all the lights out in the apartments—the silence indicative of human beings praying that the *things* out there would somehow, by some miracle, pass them by. The darkness had a lot of prayer in it, and a lot of weapon fire, and not much else—and it was uncertain to Ari which would do the most good in the long run. For preference, he would depend on the guns.

"Got a bad patch over here, Boss," said one of the voices in his armor's earphones. That was Mary, a captain and one of his sub-team leaders. She sounded more cheerful than worried. Ari grinned, firing around the corner he was stuck behind. That tone of voice, when stuck in a tight spot, was one of the traits he used to pick his teams.

"You pinned down?"

"No worse than usual. I could use some help in a while." There was a flash as she disposed of a grenade, and some aliens, and then another grenade to keep honest any other aliens who might have been behind the first little party.

"Noted. Mihaul?"

"You rang, Boss?"

"Gimme a sign."

An abrupt set of blasts at an alien said M in Morse code. It came from off to Ari's right, up past where the café had been, half-sheltered under a sign that had said PANETTERIA and now said P ETT R, punctuated with blast holes.

"Good. How you doing?"

"Got you some nice cold cuts here, Boss. Her Nibs's gonna be pleased."

"Let's not count the chicken before it's home in the fridge, OK? And don't despise the live free-range livestock if you can catch any. Meanwhile, get your butt over by Mary there and make yourself useful. She's got a few too many hands for bridge at the moment. You see the front doors of the church? Those big bronze ones."

"Got it. On my way with the bridge mix," Mihaul said.

Ari pulled back from the corner for a moment and took a breath, staring out at the alien ship. The few aliens that had been close to it were dead now. Some that had broken away immediately after the X-COM team arrived were now lying helter-skelter about the cobbled pavement, the "cold cuts" Mihaul had mentioned. Some of his teammates occasionally ragged Mihaul for not firing as much as he might, but Mihaul firmly believed in not firing until he was sure of his target and referred with amiable scorn to some of his teammates' spray-gun weapon firing as "premature ejaculation." His own technique had been gaining converts lately, both by evidence of its success and as a result of Ari's—and the commander's—open approval, with the result that Ari's teams' attacks were sounding a lot less like a Yugoslavian cease-fire. His method also worked better and saved money—which counted with the commander, as well.

Now, though, Ari was thinking more about killing the rest of the aliens loose in the square than about the value of weapons charges, or the valuable elements in the alien craft, or the possibility of live captures, or anything else. One of an X-COM assault team's duties was to drive home to the aliens in the simplest possible language that terror raids were simply too costly to continue, either in terms of personnel or materiel. You did this by killing or catching every one of them, taking home every scrap of their stuff that could be used, and depriving them of everything else they had, whether it could be used or not. But mostly you did it by the killing.

The problem, here as in many other terror spots, was that the aliens loved to attack by night—and the night was their friend. Almost all of them could see better in it, unassisted, than humans could even with artificial augmentation. It gave them an advantage Ari hated, and refused to concede. He was not going to concede it now.

"Elsabet?" he said. "Report."

"Over here behind this giant tit, boss."

"That's a mausoleum, you big dumb *nyekulturnyi.* Haven't you ever seen a mausoleum before?"

"Oh, a tomb," Elsabetta Yanovna said. *"I know tombs when I see them, Boss, and I don't wanna be in one just now. Even pretty ones like this—"* She broke off, and there was a brief flare of cannon fire. Ari saw something down the road blow up most satisfactorily.

"Watch where you point that thing," Ari said. "There's an empress buried in there, for goshsake!"

"Won't bother her none," Elsabetta said, *"not the noise, anyway."*

"You may have a point, but just—" Another burst of cannon fire. Ari was glad Elsabetta had nothing heavier than an auto-cannon at the moment. Her tendency was to use the complete destructive ability of whatever you gave her, and to "let God sort them out" afterward. Ari could imagine the results of Elsabetta with a heavy plasma tonight —mostly God sorting out a lot of irreplaceable late-Empire architecture and artwork. "Oh, never mind," he muttered as something blew up even more spectacularly. What the heck *was* she hitting over there? Whatever it was, it gave more light to shoot aliens by. A small truck, Ari thought.

"People, target the vehicles. The light won't last, but it's better than nothing." He glanced over toward Galla Placidia's splendid cruciform mausoleum, with its massive dome, and spared only a brief thought for the fifth-century mosaics inside and out. The twenty-first century was his main concern at the moment.

Here and there around the piazza, vehicles began to blow up with more regularity. They were mostly just little cars, though, and most of their fuel tanks didn't have enough gas in them to last more than for a few seconds' worth of light—though that was spectacular enough while it lasted. More gunfire erupted around the square as Ari's people took advantage of the brief light, and the aliens scattered around started melting farther back into the shadows in the side streets.

Don't want them doing that, Ari thought. *I want them centrally located where we can deal with them fast.* But if wishes were any good by themselves, the Earth would long since have been free of the invaders. No chance of that. *There has to be a way, though. I don't want to get involved in house-to-house if I can avoid it.*

Ari thought hard while the firefight out in the square began to attenuate, the firing more outward than inward now. He was acutely aware of someone looking over his shoulder, as it were, listening to his comms or his teams', with what kind of thoughts he could only suspect—and he suspected he would find out.

WHAM! The blast went right past his ear, and Ari threw himself not to one side, because that would be what they were expecting, but forward, tucking and rolling fast and hard, straight over the cobbles into the piazza. Behind him, against the wall where he had been standing, something went smack, a small wet noise. That was followed by a sound he had come to recognize from too many street fights: plaster and the underlying brick crumbling as a jet of venom from a Celatid hit it, splattered, ate the outer surface, and started to work on the inner ones. That was followed by an odd little squeak as the creature got its second load ready.

Ari was already up on his knees, sighting on the nasty little sack of poison: he blasted it, and then hit the great ugly Muton that was loping along behind it, which went down and lay struggling. *Don't die*, he thought, eyeing the huge, bulging-muscled humanoid as it lay there. *We can always use a few more live ones.* All the same, he had no desire to have it get up behind him, after he'd moved on, and surprise him later. Carefully, he put a blast through each of its elbows and knees, which tended to ruin most anyone's mobility, human or alien. Then he crouched and scuttled back to the corner where he had been hiding, careful to avoid the slimy venom from the Celatid, which was still running sizzling down the wall, digesting the old, crumbling stucco.

"Report," he said quietly, watching the muzzle flashes disappear down the side streets.

"*They're scattering, Boss,*" Elsabet said. "*This batch is heading northwest.*"

"They'll hit the city wall—it's only a block behind the mausoleum. You should be able to trap some there. If you can't, though, push them around the far side and back into the square."

"Right."

"*Got a whole lot of splat-bags over here, Boss,*" said another voice. It was Roddy McGrath, another captain. "*And some Reapers. They're pushing pretty hard to get through this parking lot.*"

The Reapers were a particularly nasty threat, especially

as far as any civilians who might be in the area were concerned: fierce hungry furry bipedal things, ravenous as wolves, that would come loping along at you and rip your head off and eat it before you knew you were an appetizer. "Don't let 'em out," Ari said, "whatever you do. If you can get them to cooperate, drive 'em back up the road toward the piazza."

"Cooperate!" Roddy's irony showed more forcefully than usual. *"Might be fun to try...."*

Suddenly, a burst of plasma fire exploded from the direction of Roddy's team, down the Via Salara a block to the east of the piazza—Roddy's way of encouraging "cooperation." Ari grinned. "Mihaul?"

"We linked up with Mary, Boss," Mihaul said, cheerful. *"Not much left of the batch she was chasing. A few Sectoids are sniping from one of the apartment buildings. All the Mutons are down. A few of them are still breathing."*

"Get those snipers. Then you and Mary pitch in and help Roddy. He's got his hands full. Your losses?"

"Dagmar's down. Rio's making pickup on her."

"Dead?"

"Don't know."

"Have Rio get her home and then meet you. Go!"

Ari held his spot, watching his people work. This was the hardest part, sometimes—keeping out of their way, letting them get their job done. Behind him was the sound of more plasma fire. His own team was closing in behind him, tidying up and securing the area where their own ship had landed, in the small square at the end of the Via 4 Novembre. "Paula," he said, "got a clean perimeter back there?"

"No problems, Boss. A lot of Mutons over this way. One damn near pulled Clive's arm off, but he's still alive. Brian's taking him back to the ship."

"Other losses?"

"Nobody. Doris's link's down."

Ari raised his eyebrows. It was less trouble than he had been expecting, and comms in particular had been working well on this run. "Fine. Close in behind me. We're going to have some cleanup to do in the square in a little while."

"Right."

He leaned against the wall, watching the square. The muzzle flashes were getting closer again, coming from the side streets. Off to the left and southward, a startling *bang!* rattled back and forth between the walls of the old five-story stucco buildings and, as if knocked off by the sound, a big piece of the facing of one of them—including a couple of windows—blew outward and fell down into the street.

Then it got quiet. *"There's your snipers, Boss."*

"Good boy, Mihaul. Get your butts up by Roddy now."

"Team's there now. I did that last bit."

"Alone? You brainless—" Ari stopped, since that was exactly what *he* was at the moment—alone. "Never mind. You sure you got them all?"

"Looking at the bits and pieces right now. I'll have to count them up and take an average, but—"

"Oh, just get moving." Again he thought of that silent presence who might or might not be listening to his comms. It would probably have something to say about his being there all by himself, without even one team member for backup—if indeed it had been watching at all. It was a little like being six and worrying about Santa Claus. *He knows when you've been sleeping, he knows when you're awake, he knows when you've been bad or good....* You *think* he's watching anyway, but there's no way to tell for sure, and the uncertainty cramps your style something fierce.

The sound of footsteps approaching brought him around. It was Paula and her team: Paula in the lead, in armor since she had been hogging "point" as usual, with Matt behind her and, some ways back, big blond Doris bringing up the rear. Across the piazza, a chain of explosions went off—probably Mihaul's team laying down some grenades for cover while they joined Roddy's. Then heavy plasmas stitched the air again.

"Report," Ari said.

Paula glanced over her shoulder, the way they had come. "Twenty Mutons dead."

"Twenty!"

"We were busy," she said mildly. "I told you about Clive. He died on his way to the ship."

"Shit," Ari said softly. "All right. We've got some business to clean up yet. I want you to get your—"

He paused. Behind the rest of Paula's team, Doris was coming toward them, more and more quickly. Head down, looking staggery, looking decidedly bad. Looking somehow *lumpy*. Bulkier than she should. Running now, running at them.

Then Doris was on him. Ari saw—just before the mutated arm slammed into his helmet—her slack face, warping out of shape now, and her empty eyes. *Just barely gone Zombie*, he thought—the second-to-last straightforward thought he had before the fire became everything in the world. *God, the boss is going to be pissed.*

A thousand and three miles away, a woman sat in a small windowless office. It had a desk, two plain chairs— the one behind her desk and the one in front of it, neither any more comfortable than the other—and a door with a dartboard fixed to the back of it. The dartboard showed signs of frequent and savage use, both for normal competition—the "double" ring was thoroughly pitted— and for other purposes. Right now the center of the dartboard featured a thoroughly targeted picture of a man with a big, round, florid face and a mustache that seemed big and tough enough to jump off his face on its own and go off to seek its fortune. The picture had no eyes left: only beige cork showed where they should have been, and a dart was presently sticking, cigar-like, out of one corner of the formerly smiling and now ragged mouth.

Jonelle Barrett sat behind the desk, which was very clean and shiny, occupied only by her computer console and one piece of paper. The floor, though, was chaotically piled with paper, tapes, diskettes, cassettes, and other detritus, all bespeaking a person who preferred the least-kinetically-loaded form of filing: pile it up on the floor, where it can't fall any farther. Some of the piles (mostly the ones leaning against the wall) were quite straight and organized-looking; others were doing their best to threaten others, slumping alarmingly sideways or forward.

At the moment, Jonelle herself was taking the latter approach to life. She was leaning on her elbows over that piece of paper, staring at it, while listening idly to the chatter over her computer's comm circuit from one of the teams out on intercept.

"—keep it quiet, now—"

"—Boss'll be annoyed if we come back without any goodies—"

Jonelle smiled slightly, a one-sided, crooked expression. She shook her head in a particular way, sideways, which activated her secretary's link.

"Joel?"

"Yeah, Boss?"

"That's Five on the blower now, is it?"

"Right. They're in Tripoli."

"Give me Team Eight. Where are they now?"

"Still chasing their chicken, Boss. Somewhere over the Med."

"Where's Three?"

"Ravenna."

The smile got more crooked. "The criminal returns to the scene of the crime," Jonelle said softly.

"Colonel Laurentz take a team down there before?"

"Not a team," Jonelle said, and smiled more crookedly yet. "Never mind."

Her earpiece clicked, and someone said, *"Over here behind this giant tit, Boss."*

"*That's a* mausoleum, *you big dumb* nyekulturnyi. *Haven't you ever seen a mausoleum before?*"

Her eyebrows went up. "The model of tact, as always," Jonelle murmured.

"Boss?"

"Nothing, Joel."

The silence from her secretary's link suggested raised eyebrows, and an opinion that more than nothing was involved. Jonelle waggled her own eyebrows at the dartboard, then reached out and straightened the piece of paper in front of her.

It said:

TO: BARRETT, JONELLE, CMDR, X-COM IRHIL M'GOUN
FROM: KENNY, DENNIS, SR CMDR, X-COM CENTRAL

WITH IMMEDIATE EFFECT YOU ARE PROMOTED REGIONAL
COMMANDER SOUTHERN EUROPE / NORTH AFRICA. AUTHOR-
IZATION DOCUMENTS AND CODE KEYS FOLLOW BY COURIER.

That had been nice to read, the first time. And it had made her smile when it landed on her desk the previous week.

Thirteen months, now, she had been commander down here at Irhil M'Goun. Not what you would normally call a peach assignment. Not down here, where the major natural resources were rock and sand or, if you went out of your way looking for something different, sand and rock. Morocco was a serious pain in the neck.

Take a part of the world that held little to interest anyone, human or alien (you would have thought, anyway), dig a deep hole in it—well, several holes—and build a base. Stock it with several hundred stir-crazy scientists, researchers, and (worst of all) pilots and soldiers.

Then just sit there and twiddle your thumbs. That was what the former commander had done. Jonelle couldn't understand how anyone who had risen through the ranks in X-COM could possibly think that a base was a place that would just run merrily along by itself without serious attention or constant infusions of money. The former commander had mismanaged the place until there were chronic staff shortages, equipment shortages, even food shortages. Jonelle had trouble understanding how such a situation had been allowed to go on for so long. Whether the commander had had the fabled Friends in High Places, or whether (as Jonelle suspected) the people in High Places had simply been too distracted with more severe problems elsewhere, either way Irhil M'goun had gone quietly to hell in a handbasket, and no notice was taken...until the aliens' Good Friday terror attack on Rome.

Jonelle grimaced at the memory. Irhil had been the only base in a position, that day, to handle that particular interception. They hadn't handled it. The result had been more than six hundred dead and the oldest part of Rome devastated. What two thousand years of weathering, tourist chipping, and opportunistic quarrying had failed to do, the aliens had done in about ten minutes, leaving the Colosseum a pile of rubble and (almost as a side issue) the Pope dead underneath it. To say that the Italian government was annoyed would be somewhat understating the case.

Shortly thereafter—before the bodies were cold, Jonelle suspected—the former base commander was relieved of his command. There was a brief interregnum period of a week or so while an investigative team came down and looked the place over. Then Jonelle, at that point a colonel over in Rio, had abruptly been promoted to X-COM base commander and shipped off to run this godforsaken pit.

At the time, while not entirely understanding the rationale that had caused this sudden boon to land on her, Jonelle had been delighted. It had been a career advancement far beyond her expectations, at least in terms of time—she hadn't expected to make commander for years yet. And she was further excited because the Powers That Be plainly wanted her to act like a "new broom," in the same way she had on a lesser level with her previous commands. Jonelle had jumped into the job joyously. Now, though, she wished desperately for the good old days when she had been able to just jump out of a Lightning and blow up, with a clean conscience, anything that looked like it intended to make her day less than pleasant. She could no longer allow herself the simple luxury of handling her problems with grenades or an auto-cannon. Now she had to use balance sheets—nearly as deadly, to humans anyway, and a lot less satisfying.

The basso-static noise of gunfire rattled in her earpiece. *"People, target the vehicles. The light won't last, but it's better than nothing."*

Jonelle smiled to herself. Ari was never one to waste resources. He had been about the only one of that mind around Irhil when she arrived.

Thirteen months. Jonelle had been busy since then. She had come to a place where the tension levels seemed so much higher than they ever should at a base that was working properly. There were plenty of reasons for it, but at the bottom of them the simple fact that no one there really trusted anyone else to do their job because no one Up Top had spent any serious time making sure they did it. Jonelle sensed this very clearly but said nothing about it to anyone at first. She spent a peaceful first couple of weeks as Queen Log, sitting still and looking around to see who was using what and who was wasting it. Fighting aliens was, after all, an expensive business, and even with the whole planet in crisis, under siege by what appeared to be half of some alien planet's ecology, money to fight them still didn't grow on trees. The previous base commander at Irhil—wherever he was, and Jonelle hadn't inquired, knowing someone would gossip the info to her sooner or later—had started out with a good kitty. But he had blown an astonishing amount of it on research, producing few results and managing little successful control of that period's repeated alien terror attacks in North Africa. Jonelle had looked over the accounts and became determined to do better. There were a lot of things Irhil M'goun needed if the aliens were not simply to move in and set up housekeeping. At the end of those first two weeks, Queen Log became Queen Stork in earnest, and Jonelle set out to start shaking the place into order, and specifically to make a lot of money.

She fired a lot of science personnel who had been sitting around wasting perfectly good money and food on vague projects the former base commander had never sufficiently investigated. She started to sell even slightly outdated munitions and captured alien paraphernalia to all the anonymous bidders in sight. "I'd sell laser cannons to the Tooth Fairy if he turned up with cash," Jonelle announced, and shortly thereafter many little private flying craft started dropping out of the sky, their pilots and passengers offering Jonelle's secret civilian intermediaries all manner of hard currencies for guns and alien corpses and invaders' metal and all the other salables that successful interceptions provided. The alien corpses sometimes gave her second thoughts. *What are they* doing *with them? Using them for alien snuff movies?* It was something of a mystery. The corpses weren't a source of anything valuable, in the sense of pharmaceuticals or other chemicals, and no one she knew used them as food.

No one *she* knew. Jonelle made a wry face, wondering whether those corpses were being rendered down somehow and the components sold as instant soup to other aliens for the various subspecies that needed it. Such a discovery wouldn't have surprised her. Humans would buy anything from anyone, and sell anything to anyone. Treachery was as commonplace as honesty, and Jonelle couldn't stop it. All she could do was work to do her best for her own side.

She dug new hangar facilities and built new labs and engineering works. Then she hired scientists to replace the ones she had fired. She looked most carefully at their credentials and gave her department heads meticulous instructions regarding what researches she wanted done and how fast she wanted to see results. If they blew it, she fired them—within minutes, some complained. Jonelle let them complain. Irhil M'goun swiftly got a name as a place where someone who could produce results would be given large amounts of research space, whether they were looking at the immune systems of Floaters or neural chemotransmission in Chryssalids. It was all the same to Jonelle, and extremely talented scientists started fighting to work at Irhil. *Not bad*, she thought, *for a place that's just a bare patch in the rock.*

She started building guns, big time. "You can never have enough guns" was Jonelle's motto. Laser cannon were her specialties, mostly because of their extravagant profit margins. She sometimes wondered whose armory she was supplying—what nation might suddenly find itself with an extremely well-armed rebellion on its hands. But Jonelle entertained such thoughts only briefly. At the moment, national rebellions had to be considered mere local squabbles, compared with what X-COM and the world had to deal with. If the cost of driving the aliens off the planet was the fall of a local government or two, well...that was life. There wasn't a nation on Earth whose internal balances hadn't been thrown out of whack by the aliens' incursion. When they were gone, there would be time for the normal state of affairs to reassert itself. Of course, there would still be losses of life and other injustices, but at least people native to this planet would be the ones cleaning up the mess.

And there was always the small matter of UFO components. The previous interceptor crews had felt no particular pressure from their boss to shoot down alien craft where they could be properly plundered—a shocking laxity. There had been much too much of the "who cares, why risk our own skins, just dump it in the Med" mindset at Irhil. Jonelle had watched the interceptor crews operate for those first couple of weeks. Then she sacked almost all the colonels and some captains, started retraining a few others, and restocked the crews. Indeed, their attrition rate had already been so high that this wasn't hard. Then she personally took them out on a few runs to show them how it was to be done.

Gunfire in her earpiece, very close. A grunt—someone coming down on the ground, hard. Jonelle stiffened, listened. There was still certainly breathing going on in the background, quick but not labored. *He's OK.* The sound of plasma fire, again very close. Ari's typical staccato pattern, careful, not scattershot, not wasteful of energy. Sudden silence.

"Report."

"They're scattering, Boss. This batch is heading northwest."

Jonelle smiled again, that same slightly crooked smile. He had been a big help to her during those first couple of weeks, one of only two or three people in Irhil who appeared to have their heads screwed on the right way. Colonel Laurentz had not precisely followed her around—as some had, seeking to butter up the new commander or to find out where her weaknesses were—but always seemed to be somewhere handy when something needed explaining. That big, blond, broad-shouldered shape with the scarred face and the droopy-lidded brown eyes would be leaning against a wall in the mess, or half sticking out of one of a Firestorm's maintenance access ports, accessible, ready to talk to—easy to talk to. He had not gone out of his way (as some of the Irhil staff had done) to bad-mouth other staff or officers. Laurentz would simply state what seemed to be wrong with something, and what seemed to be needed to fix it. Then he would let you draw your own conclusions. Blame did not seem to interest him; having things work—a Firestorm, a cannon, a command structure—*did* interest him. So cool, straight-headed, and unusual an attitude could hardly avoid attracting Jonelle's attention, for she too was more interested in fixing things than in wasting time complaining about what went wrong. Soon enough, she began talking to Laurentz regularly about getting the base working properly again. Soon enough, Laurentz became Ari.

And, after a while, he became more than that. But that was his business, and Jonelle's. No one else's.

More fire noises in her earpiece—the insistent booming of autocannon—and more chat between the teams as they worked toward some common goal. *The piazza?* Jonelle briefly thought of the leave they had taken together nine months ago, while discussing private business. Ari had insisted they go up to Ravenna to see some mosaics. Jonelle, never much of an art fan, had gone along to humor him and had been somewhat surprised by Ari's profound silence in the face of the ancient, stiff-robed, dark-eyed figures laid into the walls and floors of the tomb there. She was surprised, too, to find herself moved by the haunting expressions looking at them from the far end of time: sorrowful, thoughtful—and Ari's expression, which matched theirs. A little while afterward, in the café in the street, Ari had drunk wine and filled the evening air with laughter, belittling his own response. Jonelle had smiled and nodded, going along with him. But she realized then that there was a lot more to this man than she had suspected, and that it was going to take her a long time to find out what else might be there.

If they survived, of course, for the world was not exactly the safe and stable place it had seemed before the aliens had arrived. She laughed softly at that thought: that the late nineties now seemed "safe and stable" compared to what the world had lately become.

"Paula, got a clean perimeter back there?"

"No problems, Boss. A lot of Mutons over this way. One damn near pulled Clive's arm off, but he's still alive."

He's coping, Jonelle thought, and bent her head to gaze at that piece of paper again. They had all been coping, and doing it better than ever. Irhil M'goun had finally become a viable proposition, after thirteen months of her attacking its weak spots one after another. Its manufacturing arm was doing very nicely at keeping the necessary money rolling in. Interceptions were going well. Few of them happened over water anymore, if Jonelle's teams could help it. She had taught them better. They were doing fairly well in terms of Elerium-115 pickup—better, judging by the monthly averages, than many older and better-established bases. She intended to improve that, and to go on improving her teams' response times and results on terror attack sites.

There were still things about M'goun that bothered her. Jonelle's great local worry, the lack of a mind shield, had finally been handled a few months ago. Six months back, she had hocked or sold nearly everything the base didn't really need to make the balloon payment on the screen, over the howls of protest of some of her under-officers. They had spent a lean couple of months "making do" and hanging on, financially, by their nails, waiting for the parts and technicians to arrive. Jonelle had turned into something of a harpy on the subject of economically successful interceptions, until the flight crews began to complain that she would sell her own grandmother to an anonymous bidder as an alien artifact. (The nastier of the wits added that, considering the commander's present conduct, Jonelle's grandmother probably *was* an alien— possibly a Celatid or some other poisonous old bag. And as for Jonelle—!) Yet it was astonishing how the morale of the place improved the day the screen went on. The tension in Irhil dropped off as though someone had thrown a switch. *Well*, Jonelle thought with some satisfaction, *someone did*. And it always helped knowing that your enemies couldn't hear you thinking.

Other things still needed doing, too. She wanted to build more hangar space. She also needed more research space. One of her people was doing really sterling work on Ethereals, and other scientists from all over were fighting to come work for him, but she had nowhere to put them. They needed more containment space for captured aliens, too. She sighed. *A commander's work is never done...*

Until you get something like this.

She stared at the paper. The next paragraph said:

YOU ARE ALSO REQUIRED TO DELEGATE LOCAL AU-
THORITY TO YOUR STAFF AS NECESSARY SOONEST
PURSUANT TO YOUR IMMEDIATE RELOCATION TO
SWITZERLAND FOR LOCATION SCOUTING AND BEGIN-
NING CONSTRUCTION ON NEW MAJOR BASE. PLAN-
NING PARAMETERS REQUIRE NEW BASE TO BE SITED
AND ESTABLISHED WITHIN TWO MONTHS.

Jonelle swore softly and opened one of her desk draw-
ers, where she felt around for a spare dart. It was all her
own fault, of course. She had complained, privately to
Ari, and more publicly in reports to Central, that the base
at M'goun was insufficient to handle terror attacks in central and northern Europe. Granted, attacks down this way
had fallen off somewhat after the base got its mindshield
in. But Europe had been heating up, and her teams were
badly stretched getting up there in time to do anything
useful. Yes, she knew how badly the Frankfurt and
Moskva bases had just been hit, but it was hardly fair for
M'goun to hold the bag for two continents at once. It
barely had enough resources for North Africa.

And here was her answer, in black and white. Central
had listened to her. She swore again. "Save us from bureau-
crats with ears," she muttered, "and brains. *Two* months!
Two goddam months! She sighted on the picture of the
former base commander, let fly, and hit him unerringly in
the nose.

This is my reward, for being right, Jonelle thought bitterly. *For getting this job done correctly, and whipping this place into shape. It was just beginning to work smoothly, things were settling down, it's not* fair.

And I hate the cold!

She got out another dart. "If I ever meet you in the flesh," she said conversationally to the picture, "you'd better pray there's nothing sharp nearby."

In her ear, someone said, "*Twenty Mutons dead.*"

"Twenty!"

"*We were busy.*"

Jonelle nodded. Her teams had learned good habits. Or simply relearned them. Either way, they were doing their jobs. She felt sure that some of the tension she had felt when she first came to M'goun was attributable to a lot of people feeling that they *weren't* doing their jobs, weren't being pushed past their own fears by a commander who knew what they were all there for: defending the Earth as though every battle was the last one. Any single, chance skirmish or interception could be the hidden turning point that would make all the difference to the planet's survival. The teams were missing that vital sense that they made a *difference* in what was going on. There had been resistance to Jonelle's pushing, at first, though not from the people who counted. Ari, in particular, had listened to some of Jonelle's more savage pep talks to her flying and fighting teams and had come away with an expression of silent, grim approval, the look of a man who has wanted to say something similar to his teams for a long time, but has lacked the support from

Higher Up. That support, Jonelle knew, meant everything to a base. A base with a lackadaisical boss gets nothing done, loses its purpose...dies under stupid circumstances.

Whatever happens, that's not going to happen to my people.

But, oh God, who the hell am I going to leave in charge here?

And then, in her earpiece, the scream. Very close. And another sound, a kind of shocked grunt: Ari. The sound she had heard him make when surprised or badly hurt. Silence—

—followed by an explosion that blew the connection dead.

Jonelle sat very still behind her desk for a few seconds. The connection did not come back. "Joel?" she said.

"Lost it, Boss."

"All right," she said, as though nothing was the matter. "Reestablish when you can. Call down to the library—I need some maps. Europe, at one to fifty-thousand, and some big-scale ones of Switzerland. One to ten-thousand, if they've got them."

"Right, Boss," Joel said, very softly, and cut the connection.

Jonelle laid aside the second dart, felt around for a pen, turned over that piece of paper, and very deliberately started to make two lists. One was a list of people she would take with her when she left—tomorrow, or the next day—for Switzerland. The other was a list of officers who might be trusted to take over the handling of Irhil M'goun while she was away.

She started to put Ari's name on the first list. Jonelle stopped, looked at it, and at the second list. Then she most deliberately put them both aside and started to make a third one, a list of projects for her new sub-commander to start work on at M'Goun. *There's going to be a lot to do here*, she thought, and ignored the way her eyes were starting to sting.

The light was everywhere. For a moment there wasn't anything else, just that and the heat, a great wash of it, and a smell of hot stone and cloth and metal singeing. Ari blinked, trying to figure out which way he was facing. Up? Down? He still couldn't see.

Something grabbed him from behind. He struggled briefly, but then got a glimpse of the right color for an armored suit: Paula, of course. She was yelling, "Get the Chryss! Get it!"

Ari blinked hard, able to see some shapes and movement now, though not much of it in the dimness. One of Paula's other armored people—probably Matt—must have been carrying a rocket launcher with an incendiary round loaded. "What the hell was he thinking of letting it off at such close range—"

"Better fried than wind up as a host for one of *those*, Boss," Paula said. Ari looked around and saw what she meant. The blackened, burnt shape that had been poor Doris before a Chryssalid got her now lay on the cobbles, straining and squirming like a horrible pupa of some giant moth. The seared skin split with a sound like tearing paper. In a shower of thin, serous fluid and boiled blood, out burst another crablike Chryssalid, young and hungry. Snarling, its claws snapping, it jumped right for

Paula. It never saw Matt, standing off to one side with something a little more suitable than a rocket launcher. The smaller auto-cannon incendiary rounds hit the monster, stitching it in four or five places in front. So many of them hit it so close together that a pyrophoric reaction began. The Chryssalid simply burst into one hot flame, burnt fiercely for a moment, and then blew itself to pieces, the pressure of the interior organs shattering the fire-damaged carapace outward.

The fumes and smoke choked Ari for a moment while he shook loose of Paula. "Thanks," he said.

"Hey, think nothing of it," Paula said as the rest of the team gathered around, all looking rather scorched around the edges but otherwise none the worse for wear. "What now, Boss?"

"Let's go help the others. They're working up toward the top of the piazza. Any more Chryssalids behind us?" Ari looked back the way Doris had come.

"Don't think so," Paula said, though she sounded doubtful. She was plainly thinking what Ari was: none of them knew how or when the Chryssalid had hit Doris.

"We'll find out in a few days," Ari said, grim. "Meanwhile we've got other problems. Plenty of our cuddly little friends up that way at the moment, and I want to make a clean sweep of them."

"Wouldn't mind some more light," Paula muttered as they headed around the corner and into the square.

Ari grinned and gestured to Matt, who picked up Ari's heavy-plasma weapon from where it had fallen and tossed it to him. "I've got an idea about that," he said. "You guys stay close to me. See the big church up top there? That's where I'm headed."

"Bad moment for an upsurge of religious feeling, Boss," Matt said as they headed up through the square.

Before Ari could answer, plasma fire rained down around them from a window up on their left. It was one of those snipers that Mihaul had missed, Ari thought. Matt lifted that rocket launcher again as the others scattered. He took aim, waited, fired.

The front of the building fell off. "I really love that," Matt said, catching up with the group as it reformed.

Ari sighed. "There was a great pastry shop in there."

"First religion, now food," Paula said, and chuckled. "Boss, you're a fickle one."

"Religion first. Come on."

They made their way up through the square, past the now-disabled alien Terror Ship, picking their way over burned and crushed café tables and chairs, and around many bodies, both human and alien. Ari was pleased enough about their response time on this one: they had been no more than five minutes behind the alien craft, though he would have preferred to force it down outside the city. *Still, just good luck that we were in the right place at the right time. If we'd had to come all the way up from Irhil on this run, none of this would be left now. None of that, either....*

He glanced at the church. Muzzle flashes and the reports and billowing explosions of grenades were thick off to the right side of it, near the head of the Via Alighieri. But there were no flashes any farther down.

"Who's holding the corner there?" he said down the commlink. "By that pale-colored building?"

"Us, Boss," Roddy McGrath's voice came back. *"We've got a good bunch bottled up here. Some trapped behind the big church, some others between it and the stone tit."*

"Good. You hold 'em there. I'm gonna get you some light to work with."

"Gonna get the moon to rise this late, Boss? Nice trick," said Elsabetta's voice.

"Not quite. Just hang on."

All around them, it began to rain white-hot fire from plasma rifles and God knew what else. Ari and his team zigzagged their way up the piazza, and all around them shots hit the burnt-out cars and soot-covered, upended café tables. Cobbles were kicked out of burning mortar by the plasma fire, and any stone not made of igneous rock to begin with immediately blew up, splintering with the heat. Fragments flew in every direction like some kind of primitive flechette grenade. Ari dodged and jumped and cursed when splinters glanced-off of his armored legs. One struck him squarely somewhere rather more embarrassing, but there was nothing to do about it but keep running.

They were getting quite close to the church, but as they approached it, the downpouring fire got so serious that Ari and his team were forced to take refuge up against the buildings on the left side of the square. They stood in front of what used to be a department store, now wall after wall of broken plate glass and shocked-looking, blast-denuded mannequins. "They're up there, Boss," Matt said, jerking his head up at the church tower, another of the low domes that seemed popular in this part of the world. "No one's going to get anything done until we get that bunch killed."

Ari breathed in, breathed out. "Damned Sectoids. On the dome?"

Matt was already limbering up his rocket launcher. "Yup."

"OK. See that rectangular bit sticking out there, on the left? That's the church's chancel. Don't hit that. When you fire, make sure the debris doesn't fall on it."

"You got relatives in there, Boss?" But Matt was loading up already.

"I'll explain later. Just keep firing. I've got something else to do." Ari stared around him for a moment, wearing what must have looked to his team like an oddly quizzical expression. "Listen," he said, "any of you have a couple of hundred-lire coins?"

Paula, through her armor's thick faceplate, and all the rest of them from under their helmets or eyeshades, looked at Ari as though he had just landed from Saturn. He looked back, and after a few seconds—one after another and with all kinds of bemused expressions—they began to check their pockets.

"I've got a dollar—"

"Uh—I've got eighty dirhams, fifty francs, and a Kenyan shilling."

"Sorry, Boss. I don't usually bring my wallet on these shindigs. I always figure somebody else'll pay for the drinks—"

"Never mind," Ari said. "I'll fake it. Matt, start firing. The rest of you, cover me too. Don't you stop until— you'll know when." And he shouldered his heavy plasma and plunged off across the piazza, toward the church's bronze doors.

They were not his main objective, but they were where the best cover was. Under the massive, arched tympanum sheltering the main doors, no fire could reach him from above—assuming he could reach the tympanum. Behind him, a number of indiscreet burping noises, like a giant paying the price for bolting his nachos, suggested that Matt was getting into his assignment. Above and behind Ari, burning stone and ancient brick leaped away from the dome. Above the noise of the explosions, he thought he heard a couple of screams in the little high voices of Sectoids. "Good," he muttered to himself. There was something particularly satisfying about shooting Sectoids, with their sinister looks, like dark-eyed elfin children stolen and turned into something sinister and deadly. Ari paused by the last street corner, across from the brick walls of the church, getting his breath for the big run across the exposed space. "You guys in the back," he muttered down the link, "that light is coming up. I expect you to drive all your targets down into the piazza. Matt, when you finish with the dome, you and Roddy's bunch get ready to turn all your attention to the middle of the piazza, between the church and the tomb. About thirty seconds. Ready?"

Acknowledgments came from one team leader after another. "Matt," Ari said, "*hammer it*—!" And he ran out into the open.

The Sectoid snipers above had little time to get off more than two or three volleys of plasma bolts before Matt's really serious attack on them began. The old brick cornices around the dome practically leapt into the air, raining down into the piazza. *Miss the chancel, miss the chancel!* Ari thought as he ran desperately, zigzagging again, for the shelter of the church's tympanum. Thirty yards—twenty—

He was under, in cool black shadow, looking out into night only occasionally lighted by weapons flashes and explosions. Ari paused, listening to the tempo and ferocity of the fire increasing from the back of San Vitale's Church, as the other teams started to drive their assailants around front. *Better move now, before they come around the church and find you right out there in the middle of things.*

Ari sucked in one last deep breath. Odd, how sweet these frantic breaths could taste, when you weren't sure you were ever going to get another one. He ran for it, up the piazza and to his right, across the empty space and toward the massive iron-grille gates of Galla Placidia's mausoleum. Explosions in the night, shouts of the living, snarls of the dying, the sounds of alarms and excursions everywhere, but nothing came close to him, none of the flying fire came to lodge in his flesh. Ari came up against the iron grille with a clang, seized it, shook it: locked. After hours. No way to get in and under cover. *Never mind.*

Ari made his way over to the right of the grille. There it was, the plain little steel box fastened to the gate, with its stenciled message. LUMINATIO AUTOMATICO, 200 L.

Ari shook his head with a look both bemused and grim. "Sorry, guys," he said, and unslung his heavy plasma. With the greatest possible care in this darkness, he shot one corner of the box off.

Heat and the stink of molten metal and scorched paint flew up in his face. Ari choked and waved the smoke away, then bent and felt about at his feet. "Ow, ow, ow, oh, shit!" About half the coins that had fallen out of the coin box were molten, and lay scattered around in little pale puddles on the pavement. "Goddamn gun!" After a moment, though, he found one of the last-fallen hundred-lire coins, which was still intact, and then another. "Awright," he said, and straightened. He put them into the coin slot on the top of the box, praying that he hadn't destroyed anything important. One coin in, push the plunger. The second coin in, push the plunger.

And wait...

And wait...

Then, sudden glory, as though the sun had come up in the piazza: a blaze of pinkish-colored sodium-vapor light burst out from ten different sources, so that the front of the mausoleum and the front of San Vitale's Church and the piazza in between them turned into a shining space burning in the red of brick and sandstone, the white of anciently quarried marbles. The town council had really done themselves proud on this lighting installation, as Ari had remarked to Jonelle not too long before. The spotlights were set up on some of the buildings surrounding the piazza, and some were set into the ground in front of the mausoleum and in front of the church, turning the whole area, in a blink, from a dark and dangerous open space into a well-lit shooting gallery for his people—a space now abruptly filling with aliens being forced into it, for his people had taken him at his word when he told them "thirty seconds."

He took a moment now to shoot the chain and lock off the grille-door in front of the mausoleum so that he could tuck himself into the low, arched doorway there and fire from cover. There was almost no need, for all hell was breaking loose out in the middle of the piazza. Plasma and laser blasts darned the air from four different directions, grenades flew, and stun rods crackled and zapped. In the midst of this chaos, stately and gleaming, the architecture of Byzantine Rome looked calmly down on the carnage. This *son-et-lumiere* part of the operation lasted no more than another five minutes, and finally the firing started to die away, the grenades exploding no more. It was just as well, for after six minutes—as Ari knew would happen—the lights went off again. You only got so much light for two hundred lire.

He sighed, chuckled, and went out to the fallen coin box to get another couple of coins. When the lights came back on, his teams were beginning to reassemble in the piazza, taking stock of the aliens they had stunned and captured alive. There were some Mutons, dumped in a muscly heap like a bunch of green-skinned professional wrestlers, and a Sectoid leader, semiconscious and lying helpless, like a drugged child, while being secured. Others of the teams were assessing their own casualties. One of Roddy's team was dead, his head blown off. Mihaul had a bad leg burn from a plasma rifle, self-cauterizing as usual, but there was always the danger that the victim would go abruptly into shock. Fortunately, Mihaul showed no such signs as yet. He was pale, but hanging on all right, and would make it home to Irhil without too much trouble, Ari judged.

"Nice job, you people," Ari said to them as they gathered around him. "Nice job. Her Nibs is going to be seriously pleased with us when we get home. We get all the Chryssalids? You sure?"

The teams gathered around him were nodding. "Not that many in this batch, Boss," Roddy said. "I'm sure we got them all."

"OK. Call home and have them send up a stripping team for this Terror Ship. We'll take the important stuff with us. Paula, go in with another suit and get the Elerium out of that thing. The usual pickup on discarded weapons: take anything big or obvious. Then post a guard. The strippers can salvage the rest, and they should be here before the rest of the town turns out for souvenirs or to pick up a little bargain. Anything else need doing?"

Heads shook all around. "Nice job," Ari said again. "We saved the world again tonight. Let's clean up here, and then go home and have our dinner."

The teams began to disperse, going about their tasks. A few stayed with Ari for several moments. "Nice trick that," Elsabetta said, "with the light. How'd you know that was there?"

Ari smiled, thinking of Jonelle's face in the light of a little wavering candle in a glass, out here in the piazza not too long ago. He also thought that there were some things a team commander should keep to himself. "Hey," Ari said, "when you go somewhere new in Europe, don't you read the Michelin guide first? You're missing all the good stuff. Get the green one."

Elsabetta snickered. She and Matt and the others stood a little longer with Ari, just breathing the air, all quiet now with that particularly terrible silence that falls after a firefight. "Whose church is this, Boss?" Matt said, looking up into the church's tympanum, which was no longer shadowy. Up in the arch, ranks of carved, brightly painted and gilded saints, choirs of angels, and herds of fabulous beasts looked down at them with incurious eyes. "It's really something."

"Various people had a hand in building it...but most of this work was the Empress Theodora's, originally." Ari couldn't help but smile. Theodora had been the religious type only insofar as it served her purposes—but when she built a church, she *built* one.

"No, I mean what saint?"

"Saint Vitalis," Ari said.

Matt blinked. "Something to do with barbers, right?"

"Matt," Ari said with great affection, "you are living proof of the triumph of popular culture and the decline of the classical education. As though it matters while we're having an alien invasion. Come on, let's get all our people together and go home."

Two

S o let me get this straight," Jonelle said to Ari, two hours later in her little office. "You went out into the middle of an open space under attack by hostiles, without backup, without even one team member to back you up—"

"They were covering me!"

"Not that you told them what for. I'll come to that in a moment—"

Ari doubted she would. This debrief had not exactly been turning out the way he'd intended. He'd brought his teams home with minimal losses, he'd brought back a tremendous load of equipment and salables, and he'd expected at least a pat on the head. It hadn't turned up yet.

"I did play back the transcripts," Jonelle said while she sat behind the desk, and Ari stood very straight in front of it—and sweated. She had her command persona very firmly in place at the moment, and there was no hope for him except to keep his mouth shut and listen. "On the off chance that there might be something in them to exonerate you for this kind of behavior. A clout on the head or some such. Unfortunately, nothing of the kind turned up, so I must assume that you did what you did while in control of your faculties. Very sad, since right now I need people around me with their brains about them, and you seem to have gotten rid of yours during our last garage sale."

Jonelle flung her hands in the air. "This is no time to discover that I can't depend on you to behave like an officer instead of a rookie. Tomorrow we have to go to the goddamn land of snow and ice, and I have to take you with me because I certainly can't leave you here after your performance yesterday, which doubtless looks like wild heroism to your poor deluded teams, who would only encourage you to do more of the same, and get you killed, which might not matter that much except that you'd take the whole lot of *them* with you. No, I've got to go haring off north with you and a few others, and we have to go scouting for some bloody half-excavated hole in the ground to stick a base in. *In two months!* Not that we can tell anyone what we're doing, mind you. We are going to have to set up an office somewhere in a new country and convince the locals to cooperate with us even though we can't and won't tell them what we're really up to. And someone is going to have to *run* that office. I have just about decided, for your sins, that it should be you. The only thing that remains for me to discern is whether or not you are sane enough to be trusted to feed yourself with a blunt spoon, let alone to be left alone with a loaded fax machine. Do you understand my concern?"

"Commander, I—"

"Colonel. Let me get very straight about this with you. I don't care two farts in a high wind about the details of your personal psychology. It must be at least tolerable, otherwise they would never have let you into X-COM. But I have had it up to here with your goddamn gutsier-than-thou behavior and your tendency to indulge yourself in these damn death-or-glory stunts. You endanger your teams by not explaining your game plan to them, you endanger yourself by doing dumb-ass things that the merest rookie would shudder away from, and by both of these actions you endanger the civilians we are supposed to be protecting. Now what holes you allow to be shot in your flinty hide I don't care in the slightest, but when you put your teams and the civilians in danger, I get cross. Cross. Is some of this beginning to penetrate the layer of ablative that surrounds your alleged brain?"

"Yes, Commander," Ari said, very evenly.

"Good. I will be watching for evidence of this in the near future. And by God, if I don't see it, I am going to pull so many stripes off your uniform, you're going to find yourself wearing a tank top in midwinter." She looked disgusted. "Winter," she said. "Horrible. All right, Colonel. My hat is off for the moment, unless you have anything to add."

"No, Commander."

"OK. Then sit down and help me look at these god-damn maps."

Ari sat down and looked across Jonelle's desk. It was invisible—unusual for her. Usually whatever she was working on stayed on her desk only one piece at a time, and when she was finished with it, wound up on the floor with everything else. The biggest map, the one of the whole country, was more or less buried. Jonelle pulled it out.

Ari whistled. "Look at the engraving on these," he said, though still in a rather subdued mode. He felt somewhat scorched around the edges. "Don't these people have lives?"

"Sometimes I wonder," Jonelle said, sitting down again and peering across the map. It was most beautifully rendered, all the more so because the mapping technology was absolutely up to date, with laser- and satellite-guided scanning and drafting. But the map still looked like a work of art, its shadings of valley-green, mountain-gray, and glacial-blue sliding one into another with tremendous delicacy, with contours in places so close together that Ari could barely see them. "Well," Jonelle said, "here we are. We have carte blanche from the national government, so the Upper-Ups tell me. We can build anywhere we like. Where would *you* put a base?"

"This is a sleazy attempt to pick my brains and let me make up your mind for you."

Jonelle smiled at him with eyes slightly narrowed. The look told Ari that, as usual, the Commander already had her mind made up, and was expecting him to reveal any weakness in her plans that she had missed. It was a game they played nearly every day, in one form or another, and Ari loved it when he won.

"OK," Ari said. He leaned over the map too, considering it as a whole for a moment. "Forget the lowland sites," he said. "But those mountains...."

He trailed off, musing. "Did you know," Jonelle said, "that the shape of the country is the basis for the Chevrolet logo?"

Ari blinked. "This?" The country was vaguely four-lobed, and longer from side to side than from top to bottom, but to call it a Chevrolet logo seemed a stretch. "You mean the cross-shaped thing?"

"Yup."

"Weird."

"But true. Chevrolet was Swiss."

Ari shook his head. "The only thing cross-shaped I can see about the country is this." He traced with one finger the long complex of deep valleys that ran from just south of Lac Léman nearly over to the Austrian border, and the north-south valley complex stretching more or less from Zürich in the north to Locarno and the border lakes in the south.

Having done so, he paused and peered a little more closely at the place where the arms of the cross would intersect. "Those are mountain passes, there, aren't they?" Ari leaned down to look at the names. Sankt Gotthard, Furkapass...."

"That's right." Jonelle was leaning back in her chair now, and she shook her short dark hair back and eyed him, smiling still. "Why no lowland sites?"

"Too easy access."

"The aliens are hardly going to rent a bunch of Chevys and drive up to the front door."

"I mean for the locals. Who needs extra attention that you can avoid? But this looks like a good spot, somehow."

"Somehow! Well, so it might. That's the crossroads of the main invasion routes for central Europe, right there. Everybody going north to south passed through there, eventually, from the Romans on...and it also became popular for the east-west route later, when the barbarians came through from both sides—"

"Hannibal came through, as I remember," Ari said, "and used vinegar to break the limestone rocks."

Jonelle smiled slightly. "The only time I know of," she said, "when vinegar has ranked as a high explosive. Anyway...control that crossroads, and you control all the other passes, indirectly."

"Though road access is hardly an issue, as you point out," Ari said. "So there have to be other reasons why you like the spot, which obviously you do, and it has to be more than mere historical significance, no matter how much vinegar is involved."

He bent over the map again. "Well," Ari said, "mountains have advantages. You're up high. The view is good. You can see anyone coming a long way away."

"When an alien ship is moving at five-thousand K.P.H.,

our detection equipment is a little better than visual," Jonelle said sarcastically, "but every little bit helps."

"Something else, then...."

"Here," Jonelle said and pushed another map at him, one of a series of many folded-up ones with green-and-white or brown-and-white covers that lay piled up on the floor by her chair. URSEREN, it said. Ari unfolded it and spread it out. Most of the map's area was dominated by a structure like a long narrow T lying on its side. The T was a short line and a longer line of mountain crests, reaching over to the middle right of the map. Under the shadow of that longest crest-line, there at its end, was a clump of black dots and some small black rectangles: a town.

"Andermatt," Ari said, and looked more closely at the fine print near the rectangles. "'Kaserne...barracks', isn't it? So there's some kind of army base there already—"

"Swiss," Jonelle said. "That was one of their army's major strategic centers. They knew perfectly well how important those valleys and passes are—they were invaded through them often enough. The advantage of the Andermatt area is that there's a lot of military infrastructure there already. The locals won't be surprised to see materiel coming in and out by air—they've been used to it for decades."

"One thing occurs to me," Ari said. "The Swiss army certainly isn't going to be terribly pleased if we just turn up on their doorstep and start building a base. I thought we were a covert organization."

"So we are," Jonelle said. "Fortunately for us, so are they." She pulled over another map. "Take a peek at this."

This map too said URSEREN. It looked exactly like the other, so much so that Ari folded it and the other map to match, laid them side by side, and started doing a "blink" comparison. No more than two or three blinks were necessary to show him that the second map had many small additions in black that the first map did not: tiny rectangles scattered about the landscape, halfway up mountainsides, apparently buried in cliffs.

"This one's under the glacier!" Ari muttered. "This one's in the *lake*! What the deuce—"

"The Swiss army likes to hide things," Jonelle said, standing up and coming around to look at the map herself. "And face it, they don't have a lot of flat land to devote to army bases and airfields and so forth. What flat land they do have, they need to grow food on. So they got busy, early in the century, and started digging. A lot of these mountains are hollow. This one"—she pointed at a rectangle apparently on the north slope of a mountain called Gletschhorn—"that's full of fighter planes. They have them stacked up in cradles, like cars in a parking lot in Manhattan. They launch by steam catapult."

"How the heck do they get them back in?"

"They ship them by rail to one of the little stations down the valley here, Realp, I think," Jonelle said. "After that"—she shrugged—"it's 'need to know', and I don't. But they manage. Other mountains are similar. That one's full of tanks. *That* one's an ammo dump. All kinds of other stores, weaponry, hardware—all tucked away for a rainy day. Somewhere down here," and she looked thoughtfully at their map, "they dug a nuclear-proof base for their heads of state and senior commanders. No one knows where it is, not even the people who built it, and I'm sure it's not on even this map. They say they decommissioned it years ago. I was tempted to ask if I could use it. But such a request would have to go through the highest army echelons, and I'd sooner not annoy them. Especially since I suspect it's not as decommissioned as they say it is."

"Interesting people."

"They are. Anyway, there are a lot of these old hidey-holes that really are decommissioned—places they didn't need after the Cold War cooled off. X-COM's liaison in the Swiss government has agreed to let us have one of those, and there are plenty to choose from. We'll go up to Andermatt tomorrow and have a look around."

"Who are we?" Ari said.

Jonelle raised her eyebrows. "A strange moment to go all existential on me, Colonel."

"You know what I mean. What's our cover?"

Jonelle grinned. "We're going to tell them we're with the UN."

"They're going to love that."

"Yes. Practically the last country on the planet to join, and I'm sure they only did it because of the aliens. No mere human threat could get them to join in the last century, anyway—that old distrust of theirs of outside alliances. But then they were burned by them so many times in the past.... Whatever. Wherever we do finally settle, our cover is that we're setting up a 'neutral observation' facility to test UN cooperation with local defense forces.

Some army people will be helping us with this, though they won't be in on the secret behind the cover. We'll be setting up a small, 'overt' base somewhere in the area, and we'll have a little office, probably in Andermatt itself, to answer the locals' questions and act as a PR front end. If you're not very careful and don't start flying a little straighter on your ground assaults," Jonelle said, "I'm not kidding—you may wind up running it."

Ari made a sour face. "Yes ma'am, Commander ma'am. I'll be good. I promise."

"You'll wind up behind that desk occasionally no matter how good you are," Jonelle said, "and so will I, since a good commander doesn't send her people into any fix she wouldn't go into herself."

"Just so long as I don't have to do filing."

The look on her face suggested that she agreed with him. But she said, "We will both do whatever we bloody well have to, Ari. As usual. Including leave this nice, comfortable place, which I finally was getting to run the way it should...."

"Would it be indelicate to suggest to the Commander that this is her own fault for being so efficient?"

"Yes. But at least I can't fault where they've asked me to put the new base," Jonelle said, gazing placidly at the map. "The Swiss location is good for Europe-wide cover, as I told them. The Andermatt location is the best in Switzerland, as far as I can figure. A near- impassable gorge to the north, a backstop of very difficult peaks to the south—most of them twelve to fourteeners—a very avalanche-prone pass on our right flank, and on our left, the longest glacier in Europe."

"Sounds like a holiday wonderland."

Jonelle snorted. "Unfortunately, it is. When it's not being a garrison town, Andermatt is a ski resort. A lot of our people are going to have to ski in their spare time, as a cover."

"How they'll suffer!"

"Don't tell me about suffering, Ari. The average day-time temperature there is already down to twenty-five degrees—it's going to be an awful winter. But at least the ground-based strategic qualities of the area are plain. Air-based strategic defense is another matter, but those mountains lend us another advantage: only pilots prac-ticed in handling those air currents will be able to move at any speed there. And if we find a spot we like, we'll start practicing right away. Aliens doing low-level work anywhere in the area will be badly handicapped. Now, can you make any case for a better spot elsewhere? None of this is written in stone yet."

Ari sat quiet for a minute or two, then shook his head. "It looks sound."

"Thanks, Colonel," Jonelle said. "I'm reassured. I'm going around to inform the team I'm taking with me on the assessment run. Would you care to accompany me?"

"Delighted, Commander."

It took them about two hours to get around to every-body. Jonelle never liked to hurry when doing her rounds, at the best of times. Now, late in the evening, with the night shift settling in and the day and evening shifts mostly in the lounges, she kept the pace leisurely on purpose.

She and Ari ambled through the main lounge in the second living quarters module. The place was full of an affable mix of ranks and specialties, some sitting and reading, a few playing cards off to one side, but these people were in the minority. There was a lot of noise at the moment because there was a serious game of "Crud" going on. Around the billiards table, a crowd of about twenty men and women were yelling their heads off at two teams of four people, who were enthusiastically body-blocking one another as they took turns trying to get at one of two billiard balls and use it to knock the other one into a pocket.

Jonelle eyed the blackboard where the intricate score-keeping grid was laid out. It seemed that the squaddies were beating the sergeants, which was the reason for a lot of the noise. As she watched, two of the sergeants shouldered a squaddie onto the floor. One of them sprawled across the table and made a mad swipe for the free cue ball. Another squaddie dove across the table, rescued it, and flung it at the free ball. It was certainly an accident that the ball hit the sergeant's head instead.

"I never could get into this," Ari said, watching with a wry expression as the sergeant, amid much laughter, staggered away from the table clutching his head.

"That's why I'm a commander," Jonelle said under her breath, with a twist of smile, "and you're not." She had been one of three people who routinely placed in the top three of the Crud championships in Rio. There was no X-COM base where the game wasn't played. "Where there is no Crud," the saying went, "there is no life." Some went so far as to claim that X-COM people had invented it, even though it had actually been caught, rather like athlete's foot, from fighter pilots formerly in the British and Canadian forces.

"Can you see Rory in this crush?"

"Markowitz?" Ari looked for a moment, saw nothing, then put his head down and listened. "There," he said, glancing off leftward. "Can't miss that laugh."

They headed that way. After a moment, Rory Markowitz slid out of the crowd, heading for the coffee dispenser. "Oh. Commander—"

"That was a nice job this morning, Rory," Jonelle said to him. "Doctor Trenchard is going to be very pleased."

Rory ran one hand through his dark, curly hair and grinned. He had one of those amiably ugly faces that prevents fights just by other people looking at it, speculating about how it got that way, and deciding they don't want to be involved in anything similar. "Thought he might like that little parcel, ma'am," he said.

"Well, so did I." He had single-handedly captured not merely one but two Ethereals while out with the team he commanded in an interception and ground assault that morning, down in Sudan. Jonelle was very pleased with Rory, as well as pleased to see him still alive. The assault had been a particularly bad one, out in an open plain with no cover of any kind. "So I've got a little parcel for you. Better run up to the quartermaster's office tomorrow morning and get yourself some colonel's stripes in time for the A.M. briefing."

That grin stretched right across Rory's face. If it could go any farther, the top of his head would fall off. "Whatever you say, Commander."

"Don't you look at me that way, Colonel. Our staff strengths support the move, and you've been a captain more than long enough. Besides, there are going to be some other changes, and I want you where you'll be able to do the most good. *Capisce?*"

"Uh, I think so, ma'am."

"Don't let them catch you thinking, Rory. They'll promote you." She gave him a little wave and headed off.

Ari walked quietly beside her for a moment as Jonelle worked her way around the table. "Other changes?" he said.

"You don't need to take that innocent tone with me. You know who Rory will work best with."

"Chavez."

"That's right. This time tomorrow, she'll be a colonel as well. So will Riordan. We were lucky in having a lot of ground assaults in the past few days—they make the changes I want easier. The numbers now back up my intentions very nicely."

"If I didn't know you better," Ari said, "I'd suspect you of changing the team makeups so that the results of the assaults would reinforce your intentions."

Jonelle gave him a look. "I'm not God yet," she said. "I will not under any circumstances put people in harm's way to further my own aims. But I can see, sometimes, how the dice are going to fall. And if I help them a little...it's all for a good cause."

"So who are you leaving in command?"

Sidelong, Jonelle regarded him with amusement. "The answer you're looking for is, 'Not you.'"

"Is it that obvious?"

"Is the Pope Irish?...Well, never mind. Who would you pick?"

He stood thinking while Jonelle looked through the other side of the noisy crowd, hunting a particular face. Not seeing it, she turned and made for the door. Ari came after her, and together they went out into the hall and headed down toward the living quarters.

"DeLonghi," he said finally.

Jonelle nodded, not saying anything for a few moments. Let him work it *out*, she thought.

"I thought you hated his guts," Ari said very softly. "After all the grief he gave you after you were assigned. 'I should have been Commander——'"

"He never said that."

"Not to your face. To everybody else who would hold still and listen, though. Insubordinate, self-righteous son of a——"

"He's the right man for the job," Jonelle said just as softly, "and I will not let my personal feelings get in the way of doing my job well, or seeing others' jobs done that way. DeLonghi is popular with the rest of the command-level staff. He's thoughtful, in his slightly plodding way. He has a temper, but I've seen no evidence that he lets it influence his command decisions. He knows how to think, if the officer directly above him isn't discouraging him from doing so—the way the last one did."

"And by leaving him in command here," Ari said, "you defuse his hostility—you hope. And give him so much to do that he doesn't have time for it anymore."

Jonelle sighed. "Politics," she said. "I hate politics. Intrapersonal, or any other kind. But you quickly become a political animal in this job. So will he. If DeLonghi makes the mistake of indulging his more malicious opinions while he's in command, he'll find out it doesn't work—the hard way and very fast. He'll behave, I think," she said, as they turned the corner down the long main hallway of the living quarters. "He'll do anything not to give me reason to relieve him. He hates any appearance of failure—it'll keep him honest."

They paused by a door with a doorplate that said DE LONGHI R.J., COL. Jonelle reached into her pocket, fished out a folded piece of notepaper, and carefully tucked it under the door.

"Another X-COM promotion ceremony completed," Jonelle said sarcastically while giving the briefest of salutes.

"One other I want to see," she said, "but he won't be down here. Come on."

They went back up the hall. "And you say you're not interested in my psychology," Ari said, only half joking. "I wonder."

Jonelle glanced at him. "When I'm dressed like this," she said, tugging at her uniform sleeve, "anything that serves my job—which is killing aliens who want to move into my home—is an interest, and I'll use it as a weapon against them, any way I can. Insofar as the contents and motives in your mind affect the way I do that job, they're an interest. When I'm dressed differently, though..."—she waggled her eyebrows suggestively—"I promise I won't use it against you."

Ari smiled. They walked quietly together for the next few minutes, Jonelle leading the way toward the lab blocks. And is it true? she wondered. Would I *really* not use what I know against him? True, she had access to his psych profiles, as well as to everyone else's under her command, on a need-to-know basis. Not that she'd ever looked at them. *It would be a bad day,* she thought, *when I couldn't tell what was on someone's mind just by looking at them.* So far, in neither their professional nor their private relationship, had there ever been need. But what if there was, some day?

She knew what a fine line they walked, this tightrope stretched between their physical and emotional relationships and their positions as commander and subordinate. Lesser men, Jonelle suspected, would have a hard time of it. Ari was smart, flexible, and sufficiently accomplished at his own job that he didn't feel much of a need to prove himself to the people around him. His impulsiveness in battle and crisis situations was just that, impulsiveness, not an indication of a man overcompensating for his position below a tough and capable woman who just happened to be his lover.

I think, anyway....

They passed through the first set of containment doors at the entrance to the lab blocks. "Trenchard?" Ari said.

"Uh huh. When did he ever go to bed early when he had a new toy?"

The lab blocks were almost deserted this time of night. After the containment doors shut after them, Jonelle and Ari passed door after door of dark and empty offices, and laboratories with all the equipment shut down except for the computers monitoring ongoing experiments. Lab staff did not stand the heel-to-toe watches that interception crews did, though teams of scientists and researchers took turns going "on call" to deal with new acquisitions of live aliens. Most of the researchers had been off duty for hours by this time of day. But there were always those who were too interested, or too driven, to stop work.

As they passed through the second, heavier set of containment doors, the ones that separated the alien containment unit from those labs where only corpses or tissue were held, Jonelle wondered which of the two categories Trenchard fit in best. His history was mostly unremarkable except for his involvement in a terror raid, during which he came close to being killed. Shortly thereafter, he had been recruited covertly by X-COM, under cover of a shell organization that claimed to be doing "nonaggressive" work on the alien genome series. His own pursuit of genome data on the aliens had proved less than nonaggressive—he worried his work like a dog worrying a particularly juicy bone. But psych profiling showed no ax to grind, no trauma to drive him. It seemed that he simply, almost greedily, wanted what the aliens had: a brand new biology that no one had ever seen before, which wasn't well understood, and which was a fertile field for a smart researcher who was willing to work hard. Jonelle was glad enough to let him get on with it. He was one of few scientists who hadn't been slacking off when she arrived, and since then Jonelle had found him a hard-headed and dependable source of advice on how to distribute appropriations. Too, other scientists and researchers around him tended to work harder in response to the way he worked, which was a dividend the commander appreciated.

Jonelle greeted the guard on duty, she and Ari accepted sidearms from him—no X-COM personnel worked with aliens unarmed, even when they were confined—and they walked on down the central hallway. The brightest lights in the area shone there, looking greenish through several layers of armor glass. That was "maximum security," for species that were psionically or physically the most dangerous. The side rooms, where other less dangerous live aliens were confined, lay off to both sides, and fainter lights glowed in them, both from normal illumination and the firefly lights of local confinement fields inside the cells. As they passed a series of smaller cells where Celatids and Silacoids were held, Ari peered in through the outer armor-glass windows and raised his eyebrows. "A lot of those on hand this week," he said.

"Yeah. Dr. Ahu asked me to have the teams bring him any Celatids...he's working on some kind of adaptation of their venom, a 'universal solvent.' He claims it'll eat through lead when he's finished with it. Anyway, he's already come up with a variant that the Celatids themselves are very vulnerable to."

"Useful. What do we administer it with? Squirt guns?"

"Don't ask me—that's not my table," Jonelle said as they reached the maximum-security area and looked through the thick glass window of the outer office. Inside, Jim Trenchard was working over a console, watching a series of multicolored sine waves weave themselves together on a computer screen and occasionally stopping to tap something into the keyboard and change the amplitude or frequency of the waves. Trenchard was a taut little man in his late forties, fit and wiry, going prematurely bald, but otherwise looking nothing like the stereotypical research scientist. His preferred lab wear was a worn blue coverall of the kind favored by furnace repairmen. Few central heating technicians, however, had the audience for their work that Trenchard had. In the inner office, hovering gently in midair and illuminated by the glow of a boosted psionic-confinement field, was an Ethereal. It seemed to watch Trenchard, though of course that was an illusion.

"They give me the willies," Ari said softly. Jonelle nodded. Of all the aliens X-COM dealt with, the Ethereals were, to her way of thinking, the deadliest. Others might be able to rip you limb from limb, or eat you alive, or dissolve you like a sugar cube in coffee, but the ones that could get inside your head and change the way you thought about yourself struck Jonelle as far worse. They were telepaths and telekinetics of dreadful power, easily the most powerful of all the alien species who worked with the weapons of the mind. There was some speculation in X-COM that these aliens might indeed be the top echelon, the ones "running things," and research was going on everywhere into the best way to interrogate these creatures.

They were very resistant, though—that was the problem. And that resistance, and their power, were both made more horrible by the creatures' physical reality. Except for their brains, there seemed hardly anything to them.

Jonelle looked at the Ethereal that floated, restrained, in the inner office. Except for the huge head that encased the thing's awful brain, the Ethereal looked pallid, withered, a mere husk of a humanoid shape, no bigger than a child. A terminally anorexic child, it would have been, the skin so thin that the blood vessels showed right through it like parchment. Not that much blood seemed to get out to the skinny, underdeveloped limbs. It all seemed destined for the brain, and from autopsy reports Jonelle had read, this seemed logical enough—if there was anything logical about an Ethereal. The internal organs were all either vestigial or hardly functional. They could not run a body, even this feeble, wizened one.

But something ran that body, even though the muscles were barely as thick as ropes and the trunk looked frail enough to break between your hands. Something—if only some kind of toxic will—lived behind those blind, dark eyes. As the creature floated, helpless, a chance air current from the ventilation system touched it, so that its body turned, and those eyes seemed to look slowly toward Jonelle. She shuddered. Only twice had she been unlucky enough, while out on an assault, to feel the touch of one of those cold, inhuman minds behind those eyes, and it had taken all the training the psi people had given her to keep her from crumpling under the force that went into your mind like a knife and began slicing away at what made you human. Since those encounters, she had become a serious convert to psionic training, and when she became commander at Irhil M'goun, she had thrown all of her people into it who had enough psi talent to bend a cat's whisker, let alone a spoon.

"Right," Jonelle said, and touched the doorbell.

Trenchard didn't look up for a moment, though he waved one hand at the door. He kept his eyes on the screen until he'd watched that pattern of sines through one long cycle, about thirty seconds' worth. Then he straightened up, rubbed his back—which must have been aching if he'd spent much time in that position—turned around, and saw who was waiting. Trenchard grinned a little sheepishly, came over to the door, and opened it.

"Sorry, Commander," he said, "I was up to my ears in something just then. How are you, Colonel?"

"Doing OK, doctor."

"Jim," Jonelle said, "we've had a little surprise from the Great Upstairs. I've got to go up to Switzerland tomorrow and start building a new base. I'm going to need to start a new research department there, and I'd like you to head it."

Trenchard's mouth dropped open. Then he laughed out loud for sheer pleasure, the kind of sound you might expect from a small child let loose in a candy store. "You're serious? You're serious!"

"Even for me, it's late in the day for jokes," Jonelle said.

"Switzerland! Anywhere near some skiing?"

Ari guffawed. Jonelle gave him a wry look and said, "We're looking at Andermatt."

"Haven't been there, but I hear it's nice," Trenchard said. "Unspoiled."

"You let me know. Meanwhile, I'd welcome an auxiliary opinion on how the sites we're going to look at will support the kind of research establishment we've built down here. Or rebuilt, I should say. Will your work permit you to leave it with your assistants for a day or two? Three max."

"That many, yes," Trenchard said. "More would be a problem. Two would be best."

"We'll plan on that, then. A transport will be ready to pick us up at oh-eight-hundred. It'll drop us at the commercial airport at Agadir. We're covert on this run, so dress and pack accordingly. There'll be a briefing pack waiting in the terminal in your quarters."

"Right, Commander."

They all paused for a moment to look at the still, drifting form in the inner office. "How's it going?" Ari said. "Is this part of that new interrogation routine you were working on?"

"This? No. This is all diagnostic investigation. I'm trying to work out where the energy to run that brain comes from."

"Any luck?"

Trenchard let out a single breath of laughter, a harassed sound. "No. The input-output figures for the creature's metabolics have never made any sense on any level, either in terms of available chemical or gross energy, no matter how you twist them. The illogic of it is beginning to affect some of my colleagues, I think. One of them went so far as to suggest in a paper that Ethereals have a 'metabolic extension into another dimension.' "

Ari raised his eyebrows. "Whatever that means."

"Don't ask me, because I haven't been able to figure it out either. I've been doing some work on ATP/ADP transport in the Ethereals' cells, but as usual there are no close analogues among the other alien species, so all the lysine-lysoid work has to be started from scratch, and—"

Jonelle laughed and held up a hand. "I'd as soon you'd write me a précis," she said, "because if you tell me now, I'll lose it. I've got about eighty things to do before I turn in tonight. We'll see you in the morning, then."

"Right, Commander. Thanks!"

"Good work is its own reward, Jim," she said. "You brought it on yourself. Good night!"

They left; the door went solidly thunk behind them. Jonelle and Ari walked back up the hall, returned their sidearms to the guard, and went out into the open side of the base again. "Amazing," Ari said after a while, "no matter how many times I go in there...I always breathe better after I come out."

"Me too. I didn't mind killing them...I didn't mind catching them and turning them over to the White Coat Brigade. But the thought of spending serious time with them...." Jonelle shook her head.

"We're just not suited," Ari said, "we simplistic, basic, emotional types. Give us a gun and a place to use it...."

"What you mean 'we,' *kimo sabe*?" Jonelle said, laughing. She laced one arm through Ari's, and they headed off toward the living quarters.

Ten hours later, and twelve hundred miles north, they stood, separate again, under a bitterly clear blue sky. It was thirty-four degrees Fahrenheit, or one degree Celsius, and as far as Jonelle was concerned, no matter how you did it, even in Kelvin, it was too goddamn cold.

They stood under the shadow of the peak of a mountain, in snow about two feet deep. Off to one side, the helicopter's rotors had slowed almost to a stop, and the wh*uff, whuff, whuff* of their turning was, surprisingly, the only sound in that still blue air. Jonelle had expected howling wind, blowing snow. Instead there was nothing but this unnerving silence, and a world all in shades of blue: hard blue sky, softer, deeper blue snow-shadow, the royal blue brush strokes of occasional crevasses, and about six hundred feet below them, the intense sapphire of the little glacial lake.

Jonelle and Ari were in civvies, which at the moment meant the kind of cold-weather gear that moderately well-off tourists might wear: boots and one-piece snowsuits in muted outdoor colors, mottlings of brown and gold and several greens. Jim Trenchard's tastes varied; he was in a fashionable but god-awful one-piecer in a shade of violent electric puce that ensured he would never be lost in an avalanche. The thing glowed like neon, even in the shade, and against the blue-shadowed snow, he positively vibrated.

Jonelle and Ari were actively embarrassed to be with him, but the fourth of their party just laughed and told them not to worry. "That's what everyone's wearing this year," said their guide, Konni. "He'll blend in perfectly."

Jonelle wondered, but said nothing about it for the moment, since their guide came highly recommended.

Konrad Egli was a liaison between X-COM and the Swiss intelligence agency, a group so secret it genuinely did not have a name, the way MI5 had tried not to, and failed. But *then*, Jonelle thought, *in the country that invented the numbered bank account, why should I be surprised at this?* The agency, in turn, had ties with the army, though again the nature of these ties was never precisely described to Jonelle, and she was sure she didn't need to know. "Just so long," she had said to Konni when they met at the airport earlier in the day, "as someone at the army knows that someone is likely to be, uh, renting one or another of their facilities...so that they don't start shooting at us one day when we come out to take care of business."

"Oh, no," Konni said, "you needn't worry about that. It's all taken care of." That was the way about half of Konni's sentences ended. His general bearing was less like that of a military attaché than that of an efficient restaurant *maitre d'*. He looked like one, too: a tall, blocky, middle-aged man with iron-colored hair and gray eyes, like a walking block of granite. His voice was gravelly, too, except when he laughed. Then you suspected it might start avalanches.

Now Jonelle looked over at Jim's purple suit and said, "Is *that* taken care of, too? How do we explain his presence up here? Or ours?"

"You're fat-cat UN officials wasting public funds," Konni said cheerfully, "renting expensive helicopters to go on a heli-skiing jaunt. The perfect cover, since any good Swiss would believe it instantly."

"What if someone sees we didn't do any skiing?" Ari said.

"You chickened out," Konni said and laughed delightedly. "Even better. They'll definitely believe *that*."

"Wonderful," Jonelle said, but she had to smile a little. "Why exactly did you want us to see this spot?"

"Look around you," Konni said. They did. Even from the strictly tourist point of view, it was a view worth seeing. Northward lay Andermatt town, a scatter of hotels and a lot of little brown and golden houses, held inside a triangle of roads. These led west down the Furkapass valley, east to the set of murderous switchback curves that climbed to the Oberalppass, and north to Göschenen and the northern end of the great Sankt Gotthard rail tunnel. Past them, above them, the lowlands of Switzerland dwindled away into hazy views of Germany. Directly westward rose the great triangular peak of the Furkahorn, ten thousand feet high, and over its shoulder, a crevasse-streaked hundred-lane highway of ice a mile wide: the Grosser Aletschglacier, oldest and biggest glacier in Europe. Beyond that, through the clear air, you could see straight to Geneva, and France beyond. South lay mountain after mountain, like waves in the sea, the Sankt Gotthard pass and the other lesser passes spilling downslope, like rivers, into a golden haze that held Italy beneath it. Then, to the east, the heights of the great north-south running mountain chains of Graubunden, behind which lay Liechtenstein and Austria, and more distant but amazingly still visible, the Czech Republic and the borders of Eastern Europe.

Jonelle nodded. "It's certainly central," she said matter-of-factly, like someone trying to resist the wiles of a good real estate agent.

"That's not so much the point at the moment," Konni said. "Tell me: can you see any signs of, shall we say, building activity in this area?"

Jonelle looked around, hard, for about five minutes, before venturing an answer. The others did the same, though she knew they were going to leave the answering to her. The trouble was that the Swiss were past masters at this kind of concealment. You could look straight at a cliff wall and not see the fiberglass fake stone that someone had built and painted to match the real rock—not until someone came along and lifted it away to reveal the iron door underneath.

"On first glance, no," Jonelle said. "But you've got to assume that anyone who might be involved in espionage would have a lot more time to study the area than we've got today."

"That's true," Konni said. "But I wanted you to look for yourself because when we investigate the site more closely, you'll want to recognize your landmarks and remember what you didn't see. All ready, then?"

Jonelle was ready enough. Wind or no wind, her feet were freezing. With the others, she climbed hurriedly back into the helicopter.

Ten minutes' flight brought them down to the little helicopter landing site near the train station in Andermatt. "Now what?" Jonelle said.

"Now we take the train to Göschenen."

"Is the Rhaetische Bahn giving you a commission on this?" Ari inquired. Jonelle gave him a look.

They all dutifully got on the one-car RhB train. It was a most peculiar little creature. The track was slanted at about a twenty-degree angle down from the platform where they boarded, and the train car itself was built at the same angle, with all the seats slightly one above the other, as though on steps or bleachers. After a few minutes of sitting and hissing quietly to itself, the train gave a strangled hoot and started down the slope.

The track twisted and doubled back on itself several times as it made its way down a steep stone face, then went over and through a gorge nearly two hundred feet deep, with a ferocious, green-white, melt-swollen river running through the bottom of it. Finally the track straightened out somewhat, and the train car pulled up and stopped, still slanted, at another platform.

They got out. "Now," Konni said, "we pick up our ride."

He led them across the platform to where something most peculiar waited on one of the main-line tracks: a little open maintenance car, painted bright yellow. If you took a Ford flatbed pickup and put it on train wheels, Jonelle thought, it would look like this. Two Swiss railway staff were standing by the little creature, holding bright orange servicemen's vests and hardhats. Konni greeted them, took the vests and hats and handed them out to Jonelle and Ari and Jim, putting one on himself. "All aboard!" he said then.

They all looked at each other and got onto the "flatbed." Konni took what looked more like a tiller than anything else, turned an ignition key, started the little beast's diesel engine, and started running it down the track, southward, toward the opening of the Sankt Gotthard rail tunnel.

Jonelle eyed the approaching tunnel with some concern, sparing only a glance for the bas-relief carved monument to the men who died building this first of the great rail tunnels. "Konni," she said, "you're quite sure nothing's coming?"

"Oh, no," Konni said, "we're on the southbound track, not the northbound."

"You're sure nothing's coming *behind* us?" Ari said.

"We're well ahead of the twelve-fifty," Konni said.

I wish I could get at my watch a little more easily, Jonelle thought as the shadow of the tunnel mouth fell over them, swallowing them up. Soon they were left with only the light of the little maintenance car's front spot, and even that didn't go very far in this darkness.

It got cold, and colder, and then, bizarrely, started to get warmer. Jim looked around him with amusement, seeing how the stones, which had been frosted closer to the tunnel mouth, were now wet, and ahead were perfectly dry and much warmer. "In these amounts," he said, "stone is one heck of an insulator."

"This time of year, yes," Konni said. "But it's early, yet. Now then...." They were about a mile into the tunnel. Faintly, they could hear, or rather feel, a rumbling—something rushing by, somewhere. "The other tunnel,"

Konni said, "diverges from this one more and more widely as we go through—it's about half a mile away through the stone, that way." He gestured to the left. "Our business, though, is over here."

He looked right and stopped. "All right," he said, "everybody out."

Jonelle blinked, then shrugged and let herself down over the edge of the car. It was about five feet down to the track bed. The others followed, and Konni, the last one out, reached for a capped switch on the side of the car, pushed the cap up, tapped a number into the revealed keypad, and slapped the cap down again. The maintenance car jerked a little, then took off back down the track, backwards, leaving them all standing there in the cold and the dark.

Konni came up with a flashlight and turned it on. "Here we are," he said and walked over to the wall. He put his fingers under a protruding piece of rock and lifted it away—

It was just a fiberglass shell, with a big metal door behind it, for which Konni produced a key. "You'll pull that back in place behind us, will you, Colonel?" he said to Ari.

"No problem," Ari said. As Konni opened the door, lights came on in a short corridor that ended in another metal door.

They went in, Ari replaced the shell, and Konni locked the door. "I'm not so sure about this," Ari said. "Anybody could just walk down that train tunnel, at night, say—"

"No, they couldn't," Konni said and smiled, and that was all he said, so that Jonelle wondered about the statement for a while afterward. Meanwhile, Konni led them down the corridor to the second metal door, and pushed the button beside it.

The door slid open. It was an elevator, a big freight-hauling one with a door on the other side, as well. They got in, and Konni pushed one of the two buttons. The doors closed.

The ride took about two minutes, during which everyone looked at the floor, or the walls, since there were no numbers to watch. Then the door opened. Jonelle stepped out.

She opened her mouth, and closed it, and opened and closed it again before saying, very quietly, "Holy Buddha on a bicycle!"

They were in the top of the mountain, and it was hollow. It was simply the biggest enclosed space Jonelle had ever seen. To the slightly domed ceiling, far above them, it had to be three hundred feet—though it was hard to tell, with the glare from the lights on the framework hanging from that ceiling. To the far side of the main floor on which they stood, it had to be the better part of a mile. That floor showed signs of having had heavy installations of various kinds on it, though they were all gone now. The huge, echoing place had that vacated feel of an apartment waiting for a new renter.

"It's the Mines of Moria," Jim said, looking up at several narrow windows, which let in a surprising amount of light, even though they were at the bottom of crevasses.

"It's the goddamn Hall of the Mountain King," Ari said, and the echo took a second or so to come back.

Konni nodded, looking satisfied. "We're about four hundred feet directly below the lesser peak of Chastelhorn, where we were standing," he said. "This is only the top level. There are four more below it, each one with a ninety-foot ceiling, all with different accesses for heavy equipment and so forth. All quite secure."

Jonelle stood there, looking around for a long, silent few minutes, considering. The others were still gazing around them, absorbing the size of the place, but Konni was looking at her, as she could well feel even with her back turned. When she finally swung around to look at him, he said, rather abruptly, "If you don't like it, I can show you some others—"

Jonelle burst out laughing. "Konni," she said, "you're out of your bloody mind. This is exactly what I need. We'll take it."

He nodded, and the satisfied, it's-all-taken-care-of expression came back. "I thought you would," he said. "I'll inform...my people...that you'll be taking possession. The upper echelons will sort out the details."

"I want to see the downstairs, first, of course."

"Of course. Right this way, Commander—"

They walked off together, Ari and Jim bringing up the rear. "And if there's any little thing we can do for you," Jonelle said, "for...your people, in return for this tremendous favor...."

As they walked, Konni lost most of his smile for the first time since Jonelle had met him that morning. He nodded, leaned close like someone about to ask a favor, and said, "Kill them. Kill every last one of the sons of bitches, Commander. *Kill them all.*"

She took a breath.

"Konni," she said, "believe me, it'll be my pleasure."

Three

Four days later, the machinery needed for building a base was swinging into action. Materiel was being stockpiled, transports were being arranged, personnel were being wheeled or co-opted from other facilities. Mercifully—or perhaps it was just one of those cruel quirks of fate that sets you up for something *really* nasty—the number of alien craft spotted dropped off abruptly during this period. These odd quiet periods happened every now and then, for no reason that anyone could understand—though everyone had theories, ranging from biological reasons to sunspots. As a commander, Jonelle had long since learned not to question these quiet times—just to be grateful for them, and to take advantage of them to improve her base's defenses. When you were building a whole new base, a few such quiet days were a godsend. Jonelle began to think there was a good chance of actually having Andermatt Base in operation within a month.

She had two main worries. First, she had seen her budget for the new base. There wasn't enough money in it for a mind shield, a discovery that gave her a new case of heartburn every time she considered it.

The other worry was that her new day job was going to drive her crazy—if not because of the clientele, then because of the way the place smelled.

The new office of the United Nations Neutral Observer Project Central European Region had been opened three days previously in the main street of Andermatt, between the Hotel Krone and the Backerei Arens, in a building that had previously been a TV and stereo store. Just as soon as it opened, a stream of concerned Swiss began coming in the door, demanding to know who was running this place and what was being done there—*they* hadn't been consulted. In a country where people take to public life the way people in other countries go for contact sports, and where all you need is a petition with a hundred thousand names to force a national referendum on *anything*, to "not be consulted" is an extremely serious matter, one that Jonelle heard about every five or ten minutes.

She did what one usually did when managing these PR "branches" of X-COM: she gave out glossy brochures that either explained nothing in particular, or explained something that purported (erroneously) to have something to do with why you were really there. These brochures were masterpieces of misdirection, and they usually fooled most of the people most of the time. To the rest of the people,

Jonelle spent at least one shift a day listening patiently, nodding a great deal, and exercising her no-better-than-college-level German. None of these helped particularly, since for reasons of both content and expression, she couldn't understand much of what she was listening to. People kept complaining to her about things that weren't her fault, like the European Union's farm subsidies, and the United Nations' interference in Switzerland. And they generally did their complaining in the local dialect of Swiss-German, a variant called Urnerdeutsch (Andermatt being located in the Swiss canton called Uri). It was very difficult to make sense of. People tended to either sing it or cough it—sometimes both. This made for more than usually interesting complaints.

Worst of all, her office was situated between the best hotel/restaurant in town and a bakery that produced bread so good it was rumored that angels came down from God first thing in the morning to get breakfast rolls and the sliced light rye. Jonelle had to sit there and listen to people going on about silage allowances and non-mandatory bomb shelters while her stomach growled, and at the back of her mind, the issue of where to get money for that mind shield kept gnawing at her.

Ari took one afternoon shift in the office, but Jonelle quickly relieved him of this duty when she discovered that his German was even worse than hers, and that he was completely tone-deaf for the local accent. Instead, she kept him busy up under the mountain, seeing about the installation of the initial space dividers for the living quarters and so forth. Fortunately, this was all modular, and would go in fairly quickly. There were other concerns, such as where the new alien containment facilities would go. Irhil M'goun had been getting short of space for a while now, and Jonelle was keen to expand their holding facilities so that live alien research could also be expanded, to two or maybe three times as much as was going on at Irhil.

During their first day's more exhaustive inspection of the under-mountain facility, Ari had found just the place for this. Down on the third level was a series of chambers hewn out of an isolated, projecting spur of the Chastelhorn mountain: Wildmannsalpli, it was called. These fifty-meter-wide chambers, carefully isolated from one another, had originally been used for ammunition storage and were designed so that if something should set the stuff off, the blast would be confined both from the other chambers and from the rest of the base. Except for multiple baffled and booby-trapped ventilation holes, there was no way in or out of them except through a long, narrow "bottleneck" tunnel where security would be easy to maintain. The whole mini-facility was completely surrounded—above, below, and on all sides—by granite a hundred feet thick. It would make a most satisfactory holding space for even the most dangerous alien.

That afternoon, near closing time, Ari came down to the PR office to brief Jonelle on how things were going. They took refuge in the back office, where they could watch the front through a venetian-blinded window but not be heard, and Ari started his briefing. To Jonelle's amusement, however, it didn't immediately concern the new base. He had spent a long time outside the front door, carefully wiping his shoes on the mat.

"There are about eight hundred cows up at the top of town," he said, examining his boot soles carefully. "Did I step in anything?"

"No." Jonelle sat down at a small desk, which was covered with paperwork and brochures and carefully written complaints waiting to be filed.

"They came right through the town. Have you ever seen anything like that before? It's like the Wild West out there. And they had bells and flowers all over them. The bells I knew about. What's with the flowers?"

"They're awards."

"What?"

"The cow that produces the most milk gets an award to wear."

Ari burst out laughing. "You're trying to tell me that was an *awards ceremony*?"

"Not as such," Jonelle said. "But those cows and most of their herds have been up in the high pastures over by Göschenen since May. This is when they bring them down, when the weather starts to turn nasty and the grass growth falls off."

"I doubt the cows care much about the awards."

"I don't know...some of them looked pretty proud."

"I didn't notice. I was looking at the big, mean guy at the front of the parade. Thought they gave him more flowers to keep him from getting jealous."

"I have news for you," Jonelle said, grinning. "That was a *she*. Didn't you look at the rear end? That's unlike you."

It was rare for Jonelle to get Ari to blush. She managed

it this time. "You seem to know a whole lot about this all of a sudden," Ari said, turning away and busying himself with a filing cabinet.

"I had a full morning's worth of briefings on the subject from the president."

"The *what?*"

"The mayor, Ueli Trager. *Präsident*, the guy who presides—where do you think we got the word? It came from here, via France, I think. Anyway, that big cow up front, that's the head cow of the herd, the *pugniera*. She's the one who enforces the pecking order, since she's at the top of it. She also scares off wolves and such."

"I bet she does. Did the president give you a yodeling lesson, too?"

"He did not," Jonelle said, pointedly ignoring the teasing. "Herr Trager did tell me, though, that there have been a lot of abductions and mutilations of cattle around here lately. People are getting very annoyed."

Ari looked thoughtful at that. "I thought there had been a worldwide drop-off in cattle abductions." He did not add, *possibly because the rate of human abductions seems to have gone up so sharply in the last few months.* That wasn't public knowledge, and X-COM was hoping that the world's governments were too busy at the moment to compare figures. The data raised some uncomfortable questions, such as whether the aliens had finished getting whatever data they needed from cows and other higher non-primate animals, and were now concentrating on the primates.

"Well," Jonelle said, "I thought so too. But now it seems like something else is going on, and I don't know what it means. In any case, I don't like it. I'm going to get onto the data-processing people at the bases at Omaha and Tsingtao, and see what they can tell me. Whether this is just a statistical blip, or something else."

Ari frowned. "There weren't many cattle mutilations in Morocco. Then again, there weren't that many *cattle* in Morocco."

"There are enough." Jonelle leaned back. "But those cows never struck me as anything special. *These* cows...I don't know. In any case, the locals are very attached to them, and it wouldn't hurt our PR effort here if we, as a 'UN organization,' can get someone, in some unspecified way, to do something to help protect their cows while also taking care of other business. You get my drift, Colonel?"

Ari looked at her. "If you mean you're going to be sending me back to Morocco tonight or tomorrow," he said, "*that* drift I get."

Now how did he.... Jonelle sat up straighter.

"You're not going to need me here much longer," Ari said. "I've talked to the construction crews all I need to— their liaison with the army is in place now. The army people, all but the highest, think our people are going to be building some kind of new installation for the Swiss— so that's settled. The basic installation schedule is just about set up. Temporary living quarters will be ready within a couple-few days, the rest within a week or so. After that we start bringing in the basic heavy stuff— that'll take another week. All those production and delivery schedules are tight, and confirmed by the supply depots in the US and China. We're lucky, this place is a natural hangar. The number-one level hangar space is almost all ready but for the doors—they're working on that. Two, three more days—four, max. After that comes conversion of the second level for hangar space, which is in a similar state, but will take more time. The concealed entrance is going to have to be widened, while under cover, to take our bigger craft. Two weeks worth at least."

"What about the conversion of the containment spaces?"

Ari looked self-satisfied. "My cubbyholes will be ready by the end of the week. They're no use to you, though, without the environmental controls and the proper security in place, and the base won't be ready for them until the third week or so. Sorry, Boss."

Jonelle breathed out and leaned back again, looking at him steadily. Outside, on the street, dusk was beginning to fall, along with the first few flakes of a snow that had been threatening all day. "We have a problem," she said.

"Local? Or back in Morocco?"

"Morocco," she said. "Business is starting to pick up again down that way."

"How many interceptions last night?"

"Six," she said.

"How did they do?"

Jonelle shook her head. "Not at all as well as they should have." This was an understatement, but she was determined not to contaminate Ari's assessment of the situation with her opinions, forceful though they might be. *DeLonghi*, she thought, *is looking like the worst idea I've had in a month of Sundays...but it might be that he's shaken by the sudden promotion and needs a little help to steady down. I intend to see that he gets it.* "Commander DeLonghi's team assignments seem to have been most at fault. I want you to get down there tonight and take up a consultative role."

"And I'll be flying missions, too, of course."

Jonelle paused. This was where she should have said, easily, *Of course.* But she couldn't get out of her mind Ari's last mission. That one had been very close. *His impulsiveness....* Yet the last thing a responsible commander in her position should do was try to shield one of her people from the correct exercise of their duties, for strictly personal reasons.

"Of course," she said. "One thing: I require you not to expose yourself to what I would consider unnecessary danger while you're in consultative mode. When you're supervising a number of teams, which you may be for the next little while, you stay out of the front line."

She watched Ari contemplating the wording of her order to see if there was some way he could squirm out of it. But Jonelle had been thinking about this for some hours. "I would do this myself if I had the leisure," she said, "but I don't. Though I can turn this office over to our PR people full-time tomorrow, there are other matters connected with getting this base running besides strictly construction-oriented ones, and I've got to deal with them." *That mind shield*, she thought, still wondering where the heck she was going to find the necessary cash for it. A shield was so necessary, up here where there were so many more people living nearby than there were in Morocco.

"Yes, ma'am," Ari said.

"Is that a wilco?" said Jonelle.

Ari looked at her for a moment, then said, "Wilco."

"Thank you," Jonelle said—something she did not have to say, and Ari knew it. "I'd be glad if you were on your way down there as quickly as possible. I can't get out of my head the idea that the aliens may have some intelligence about what we're doing...and I would very much dislike seeing our work here interrupted because of ineptly constructed and dispatched interceptions. I want my best pilot on site to advise the new commander at Irhil."

He looked at her with a flattery-will-get-you-nowhere sort of expression, but an affectionate and respectful one. "I'll be back there in a couple of hours," Ari said. "There's a transport leaving the mountain in fifty minutes—I'll be on it."

"Very well. Is there anything else construction-oriented I need to know about?"

"No, Commander."

"All right. Let me give you the details about last night's interceptions. You'll want to look at the transcripts yourself when you get back, but I think you'll find some patterns."

They spent half an hour going over the fine points of whose team had been misassigned, who needed to be spoken to about weapons allocations and armor, who was carrying weapons too light or too heavy for their best use. Outside, the snow began falling more thickly, blowing golden-colored in the light of the streetlight by the door.

When they were finished, Ari saluted Jonelle and said, "Good night, Commander."

Jonelle saw a great deal in his eyes that he was not going to express, even here when they were alone. Concern for her—and a great eager desire to get back to the things he loved best: flying his Firestorm and leading ground assaults. "Good night, Colonel," she said, returning the salute, "and good hunting. I'll expect a report first thing in the morning on improvement of the teams' results."

"You'll have it." And out he went into the snow, stopping once to look up and down the street—not for traffic, Jonelle saw, but to tell whether he was likely to step in anything bovine and unexpected.

She smiled and turned back to the desk with a resigned look, thinking about that mind shield again, and eyeing the piled-up filing.

Many miles north, in Zürich, dusk was also falling, though not snow. It was rush hour, and the rain had been coming down gently for about an hour now, drifting from one of those low-ceilinged overcasts in which the city seems to specialize in the fall. From the stone front steps of the Hauptbahnhof—the main train station—the view up the long, wide Bahnhofstrasse—the main street downtown, known for its shopping—was much shortened by the misting rain. A few blocks up, the street disappeared in swathes of silver-gray, only the stores' illuminated signs and windows blooming through the wet, drifting fog. Mist was tangled in the upper branches of even the youngest of the lime trees lining the street. The logos of the big banks facing into Paradeplatz three blocks down were mere ghosts of themselves, phantom aspirin-tablets or crossed keys glowing through the gray. Far below them, the blue and white Zurich city trams glided and hummed along the Bahnhofstrasse tracks, single headlights glowing brighter through the gloom and double taillights vanishing as they went. On either side, bundled-up people hurried along the gray and white sidewalks, heading for the tram stops or the escalators at the corner of the Strasse and Bahnhofplatz, which led down and over into the train station.

The high whine that started to become audible made some of the passersby look up, and some who were closer to the Hauptbahnhof looked back toward the train station, though dubiously. Sometimes one heard the occasional screech of wheels from the train yards, but it wouldn't be so prolonged a sound. Others glanced up the road to see if a tram was coming that possibly had an engine fault. But the trams were making no louder a hum than usual. Maybe it was just the fog. It could seem to concentrate the sound, sometimes.

But no fog could make anything—tram, train, or jet—sound like this. The whine scaled up into a scream, and the scream got louder and louder.

That was when the shape came slowly, gently bellying down out of the mist over the Zürich train station. It looked like two very large octagons stacked on top of each other, with four octagonal pods underneath. Slowly and with seeming care, it sat itself down on the stately neo-Baroque upper hall of the station—and down, and farther down, until huge blocks of stone burst out of the structure under the pressure and flew across the plaza, smashing into the hotels there and rendering some of the guests' stays unexpectedly permanent. Other fragments shot into the fairy-tale towers of the Swiss National Museum behind the Bahnhof, knocking the greened-bronze conical tops off them and leaving them like stumps of broken teeth.

At the same time, a Terror Ship settled down out of the fog onto Paradeplatz, crushing a tram underneath it. The driver of a second tram, turning the curve out of the plaza and heading north toward the Bahnhof, saw what had happened to that building and decided it might be wiser not to continue his run much farther. He stopped the tram, opened all its doors, and held his post while his passengers fled. Then he powered the tram down, checked it to make sure no one had been left behind, and jumped out himself, turning by the front door to put in the key that would let him shut the doors and lock the tram from the outside. It was the last thing he ever did as a human being. A second later, a Chryssalid's venom was blasting through his body, and the tram key fell ringing gently onto the cobbles, unnoticed.

The screams in Paradeplatz, as Floaters and Reapers poured out of the Terror Ship and descended on the terrified crowds of commuters, were echoed from the Hauptbahnhof. Not even the bulk of a Battleship was able to completely crush the iron skeleton of the great railway station, Jakob Wanner's masterpiece; but destruction of mere landmarks was secondary to the aliens' purposes.

Snakemen and Chryssalids poured out of the Battleship and made their way down the station's three levels underneath the old main building. Sirens were beginning to howl outside, the police beginning to respond, but the shrieks and cries of those in the station—both those maimed or dying under its wreckage and those being torn apart or taken alive by aliens—were louder still. On the street level, at the end of the Bahnhofstrasse, people ran desperately in all directions, looking for somewhere to hide, but there was nowhere. Stores locked their doors, but Snakemen crashed in through plate glass windows to find their prey. Cyberdiscs blasted their way through hastily dropped security shutters and racketed around inside the breached premises like psychotic Frisbees, killing everything that moved, shooting everything that didn't. Plasma-weapon fire began in earnest out on the streets, and stun bombs and grenades could be heard everywhere. Unconscious and wounded humans were carried into the waiting ships to be experimented on later. Others, more fortunate, died quickly, burned or blasted or torn apart. The gray and white pavements began to acquire a new color: red.

And in the Bahnhof, that temple to punctuality, the trains stopped running on time.

A few hours after he left Jonelle, as he had predicted, Ari landed at Irhil—and he could hear the buzz from the hangars before he ever got near them. People were running in all directions, some with pleased expressions, others with looks that suggested they felt more like the denizens of a kicked anthill.

The last thing he wanted to do was head away from the hangars, but he did that regardless, making his way to the commander's office as quickly as he could. It was very strange to knock on that door and not hear the familiar "Ngggh?" which was Jonelle's standard response. DeLonghi's voice said, "Come!" from inside, and Ari was astounded to feel a pang at it *not* being Jonelle. *No time for this,* he thought.

He walked in to find DeLonghi sitting in the middle of a desk piled high with reports and God only knew what else. The sheer weight of stuff, on a desk that he had only seen clean before, made Ari pause in amazement.

"You wanted something, I take it?" DeLonghi said, looking up and frowning. "I'm rather busy at the moment."

Ari saluted and said, "Sorry, sir. The commander—"

"Yes, I know, sit down and let's get on with it," DeLonghi growled. Ari sat down, not feeling entirely comfortable. DeLonghi had never been the easiest man to get along with. There was not precisely bad blood between them, but DeLonghi had never been that accomplished a fighter, or pilot, or strategist. There was a feeling in ranks that he was one of those who had accomplished his climb strictly "by the numbers," because he couldn't have managed it any other way. Ari suspected that DeLonghi knew perfectly well about this opinion of his peers, and that it rankled him. Privately, Ari—regarded on the base as one of their best pilots—wished that Jonelle had stuck him with almost any other job than that of having to advise this man, who would almost certainly take any advice as something meant to make him look dumb.

"What's the situation at the moment?"

"Thought you would have checked on the way up," DeLonghi said irritably.

"I did, sir," Ari said, "but much may have changed since then." He glanced at the ceiling, as if calculating, and said, "One Interceptor is in Kenya, having splashed an alien Scout Craft. Two dead, equipment and resource recovery uncertain. It appears to have been a feint. The other Interceptor is in the Peloponnese, scrambled just after the first one. Chased a medium Scout into the water between islands. One dead, and the Interceptor is on its way back here, having suffered damage. This too may have been a feint of some kind. Our Skyranger is en route to an alien landing site in the Canary Islands. The first ship we sent in, a Lightning, has been destroyed with loss of all crew. It was carrying a full load of twelve soldiers." *Who do I know who is ashes or a corpse in the Atlantic right now?* Ari thought. "Another Lightning is en route to a landing site near the old diggings at Çatal Huÿuk in Turkey. ETA ten minutes. The third Lightning is in Burkina Faso, cleaning up an alien terror site. Heavy casualties: the captain on site reports two-thirds of his assault team dead, along with fifty-odd civilians. The fourth Lightning is still finishing maintenance, should be ready tonight. Two of three Firestorms are out, one on an interception over the Mediterranean, heading toward

Egypt when last reported. The other is heading up the French coast toward Brittany, in pursuit, reporting that the alien craft, a Harvester, seemed to be making toward Great Britain but has now doubled back and may be bound for Paris or the Benelux region instead. As of my last check, anyway."

Ari watched DeLonghi go increasingly red, and he could understand why: his information was no more than three minutes' old—possibly fresher than the commander's own.

There was no question, apparently, that the commander knew this. "Colonel," DeLonghi said, "I hear the sound of a man looking to catch me in a mistake. Are you bucking for my job?"

Ari blinked. He had realized on the way there that Jonelle had sent him to Morocco in the hopes of forestalling this situation, but the aliens had had other plans. "Sir," Ari said, "if you think—"

"Because don't think that I don't know, as does everyone else here, the nature of your relationship with the regional commander. And if you think that her position will protect you when you make your move, then you've—"

"Commander," Ari said, "permission to speak as freely as you have already begun to."

DeLonghi blinked—a dreadful expression, like a cobra blinking while it had a slow, cold thought—and then said, "Granted."

Ari sat back in his chair and said, "Sir. Your materiel is spread dangerously thin. You have scattered a large force, which would otherwise have been in a position to lend itself assistance, as it were, internally, over two continents." DeLonghi's face was a study: whatever he had been expecting Ari to say, it wasn't this calm assessment. "I understand the cause of this, and indeed you had no choice. You reacted to each crisis, and logically, as it arose. But these crises show signs of having been designed to do precisely what you have—spread us out. Someone knows from experience what resources we have here. Someone may also know that there has been, shall we say, a change in management. Whether they knew before, or not, the actions of the past few hours have convinced them. Now, you find yourself with few resources left to deal with any large incursion. I would expect such an incursion to happen any minute. I've seen this happen before, when the regional commander first took over here, and the pattern—"

The klanger went off somewhere down the hall, and after it the pilots-to-hangar shouter, a melancholy hooting like an elephant sorry it ate that last tree. At the same time, the commander's phone went off. He snatched up the handset and almost yelled, "What?"

Ari stiffened, knowing what it was. *It's been three days since I've flown*, he thought. Not that that was precisely a lifetime. But three days could remove enough of your edge to kill you.

DeLonghi slammed the receiver down. "Zürich. They're in the middle of Zürich. A Battleship and a Terror Ship."

Ari was up out of his chair and had already yanked the door open. "I'll scrape the rest of a team together and get moving."

"Colonel," DeLonghi said, his voice oddly strained. "The regional commander's orders to me were quite clear. You are not to—"

"What was it you said," Ari said softly, "about protection, Commander? And positions? I'm still speaking freely. By permission." DeLonghi blinked again. "You have no one else to send. Our people are all over the place. I just came in, I have half a crew with me, the other half can be assembled in about three minutes, and my Firestorm is in the hangar prepped and ready where I left her. Not that she's likely to do any good in this case. I'll have to take the Avenger...and you might need that Firestorm for something later. Meanwhile, I can at least do some good while you get the teams freed up to back me. Pull the Canaries team back when they've finished their intercept, and the Greek team then send them along."

"I said it was a Battleship and—"

"Commander," Ari said, "screw them. Screw them right into the ground. Which I will, if I get the chance. You mentioned protection? I'm going to get out there and do some. That's my job, and yours. You have no other options, and neither do I...orders or no orders."

He grinned, and only for a moment the ferocity showed. "You wanted command," Ari said. "Enjoy. And when those other intercepts are finished with Zürich, get them back here and load them up again, because our cuddly friends out there aren't finished with us. Call Medical and get them ready, too—we're going to need them tonight. And before the others come back, whatever you do, don't send out that last Firestorm! Because...." He stopped himself from saying "she"; sometimes a pronoun could be too loaded. "It would not be typical of previous command...and besides, they'd know then that you're empty."

"Sir," Ari added after a moment.

They simply looked at each other.

"Go," DeLonghi said.

Ari nodded and went out the door, noticing—with another odd pang—that, as he slammed it shut behind him, the old half-a-second-later *thump* of the dartboard was missing.

Odd, how such little things hurt.

In the darkness around the Hauptbahnhof, silence came and went. Every now and then it would be broken by gunfire, but the sound always stopped quickly. Where there was organized resistance, it soon ceased, as armed aliens came upon it and stopped it. No city police force was equal to this kind of onslaught.

On the Bahnhof itself, the alien Battleship squatted low and menacing, while smoke from electrical fires in the station and steam from broken pipes rose around it and wreathed it in fog. Down by Paradeplatz, civilians culled from other streets were being loaded into the Terror Ship, some stunned unconscious, some dead. Snakemen and Floaters came hurrying like worker bees, bringing more and more of the human cargo.

The Bahnhofstrasse holds some of the world's most expensive real estate. There is not much residential housing there, the street being occupied mostly by stores, hotels, and banks. But in the little side streets between the Bahnhofstrasse and the Limmat River on one side, and the smaller river Sihl on the other, many apartments were tucked three and four stories up in buildings hundreds of years old. From these back streets, slowly, the sound of gunfire began again. The guns did not belong to the police.

The tempo of the aliens working in Paradeplatz began to quicken. They were used to some level of resistance, but normally this fell off quickly as the humans realized it did them no good. These humans, though, seemed slower to realize this than usual, and their gunfire was finding some marks among the less well-protected aliens who ventured down the winding back streets. As if in obedience to some overriding will, the percentage of better-armed and armored aliens foraging down those side streets began to increase. The ones servicing the ships, picking up more humans and stowing them, slowly came to the aid of the less well-defended aliens. They were safe enough—and no humans had yet been mad enough to try to approach the ships.

All this was as the aliens had predicted. Their food supplies would be well-augmented from this raid—and experimental supplies, as well. Their plan would continue unhindered.

Two hundred miles away to the east, a single Avenger was plunging through the night sky over Fribourg, heading for Lac de Neuchâtel and the Jura Mountains. It was taking advantage of the low clouds, and of being low—and it was giving Ari the willies.

"Where do you want me to turn, Boss?" said Rosie, the pilot. "Basel?"

He sat himself down in the spare chair, the fire-control position next to the pilot in the main cockpit, and shook his head. "No sooner than Colmar. Hang a right there. We'll head straight over the Black Forest, come down on the other side of it near Schaffhausen, and then low and fast, straight for Zürich."

"You got it. You want to take the hot seat then?"

"No," Ari said. "Gunnery."

"Gunnery?"

"We've got a sitting duck at the moment. If someone misses, I want it to be me. Don't want to have to blame it on any of you guys."

"The trouble with you, Boss," Rosie said, "is that you don't know how to delegate."

Ari closed his eyes and laughed, just briefly. He could remember Jonelle saying something like that, and not just once, either. "You may have something there. But this one's mine. You just fly, and be glad I'm letting you do that."

"Gosh, Boss, you gonna let us fight when we get there, or will we be stuck standing around and cheering?"

"Don't get cute," Ari said, but he was grinning. "My first interest is catching a Battleship just sitting there on the ground. I don't intend to let them just waltz off with that thing. Get on the horn—tell the captain and the sergeants I want them up here for a fast briefing."

"Yes, sir."

Within five minutes, they were assembled in the cramped cabin, and those who couldn't fit inside were at least standing within earshot. They looked at him somberly. "Is it true," one of them said when Ari called them to order, "that we're going to be the only craft responding to this call?"

Ari nodded. "Until the commander back at Irhil manages to free us up some backup. So I'm going to have to drop you people sequentially, and you're going to have to work your way in from the perimeters. I know this is not our preferred method of working, but we're short of options at the moment."

He brought the city map up on the screen. "OK, here's the scoop. We are, I believe, fully loaded."

Captain Hecht nodded. "Four heavy weapons platforms are loaded," he said, "and we're carrying twelve soldiers. Six in armor."

"OK. Take a good look at this. Here's the central part of the city—it runs down either side of the main river, the Limmat. The river veers east just above the railway station. Farther down, there are a lot of bridges over that river. Now at the moment, all the aliens are still on the east bank, as far as we know. So I'm going to have Rosie take us through town in two passes. The first one is to take out that Battleship, if God smiles on us and the big ugly thing is still sitting where it was reported. I'm not likely to get more than one shot without it knowing exactly where I am, so that one's got to count. I'm hoping that will be enough." The hope was fervent. The Avenger was carrying a fusion-ball launcher, and he had heard that one "good one" correctly placed was enough to take down a Battleship. But this was not a weapon he had worked with frequently, and there were so many variables. The worst one was that the ship was on the ground. A miss, if that ship decided to move at the wrong moment, could destroy buildings all around the strike site and kill a lot of civilians, while possibly not doing what had been intended. And then there would be six long seconds before he could reload and come about again. During which time, God only knew how many directions the Battleship would have splattered him and his people in.

He put that thought forcefully aside. "Then we have to drop you folks to best advantage. Now, the biggest concentration of civilians is going to be south of the train station. I'm sure the aliens know that perfectly well, and are concentrating on it, rather than the industrial area full of factories and train tracks that's a little farther north, or the Zurichberg and the Uetliberg, the two hills just past it. Not worth their time, and any of them that go that way will be very exposed and easy to pick off. My guess is that our cuddly friends'll be heading south, first down the left side of the river and then the right, if we let them. But if we seal off those bridges first, that'll be a big help right there. It'll confine everything but the Floaters and Cyberdiscs to this side of the water—and those guys we can hunt down later if we have to."

"What about the train station itself, Boss?" said one of the sergeants.

"That's a problem. A lot of the aliens will probably be down there right now, since at any given moment there are usually about five thousand people in it. They'll be having a field day. But they're going to have to get the people up *out* of there and get them into that Terror Ship. That won't be easy, or quick, especially since they've trashed the upper levels. It's a good thing that they won't have had time to get too many into the Battleship...which makes me feel not completely like a bastard for blowing it up. Once it's done, there won't be any more captives taken from the train station, anyway, which is probably going to be the aliens' best source."

There was a mutter from the sergeants. No one liked the idea of killing civilians they were meant to save, but all of them realized the occasional necessity. "Don't blow it completely to shit, Boss," the captain said. "Her Nibs won't like it. All that Elerium scattered all over town...."

"I'll try not to," Ari said, and fervently hoped he would somehow be able to confine the damage. But if it was a choice between utterly destroying the Battleship and attempting to keep the ship partially intact and then having it get up and go elsewhere, he much preferred the former. It would be much easier to shamefacedly say to Jonelle, "Sorry, it went off while I was cleaning it," and to take the blame for losing a lot of potential funds, rather than let the aliens have back a Battleship that they would certainly use against X-COM again.

"So," he said. "I'm assuming they haven't made it all the way down to the bottom of the Bahnhofstrasse, where it hits the lake. We can only hope. But when we make our second pass, I'm going to drop you people in the neighborhood of these bridges, on the far side." He showed them the six main bridges connecting the left and right banks of the Limmat, like sutures over a long, straggly scar. "Cross them, and secure them."

"Any preferred method, Boss?" said another of the sergeants. "There are only twelve of us."

"I know that. How do you think I meant? Just blow

'em up. The one by the station is the main priority, and the two really big ones, two-thirds of the way down, and the one by the lake. Take the others out any way you like. A few good hits with a rocket launcher will probably do it—they're not very big. Once over, I want two teams to cross the Bahnhofstrasse and start working their way up it, and through the main street paralleling it on the left side. The other teams, come at it from the right side. The middle bridge there is about on a level with where we think the Terror Ship is. It's the only place where there's really room for the thing to put down, anyway."

He pointed at Paradeplatz on the map. "The right side of the Bahnhofstrasse is part of the Old Town. It's partially residential. A lot of twisty little streets, a lot of them go uphill or downhill kind of steeply, especially over by this church with the big clock, St. Peter's."

"Residential, huh?" Captain Hecht looked thoughtful. "We've been monitoring police band. They say there's a lot of fire coming from over there—*not* police."

Ari chuckled grimly. "It's the Swiss army."

"Huh?"

"Just about every man in this country has his gun and ammo at home in case there's need for a sudden call-up," Ari said. "I have a feeling some of the locals have decided this constitutes a call-up. Good for them. Just watch your backs and make sure they don't shoot you in an excess of enthusiasm."

The team leaders nodded. "OK. The southern teams push north, up the Bahnhofstrasse. We try to get them concentrated in one place, to make it a little easier for the reinforcements when they show up. And for us, of course."

"When *are* the reinforcements going to show up, Boss?"

Ari looked at them. "Before we're finished, I hope," he said, and let them take the pun as they pleased. "We may just have to handle this ourselves—no telling."

The sergeants looked at one another. "Just passing Basel, Boss," said Rosie.

"Very good. Let me know when we hit Colmar." To the team leaders, he said, "Are we all clear on the order of battle? Blow those bridges. Then come up around the bottom of the Bahnhofstrasse and start pushing upwards."

"If reinforcements do show, Boss, where you going to put them?"

"East side," Ari said, "and they can keep the aliens from breaking out that way, and push toward us. Then more for the train station. When we've handled the ones in the streets, we're going to have a lot of mopping up to do, I'm afraid. It's just strategically sound, from their point of view, to head down into the station's lower levels. Hundreds of nooks and crannies, offices and hallways to hide in...." Ari shook his head.

"Thinking of blowing the place, Boss?" Rosie said from behind him.

"No...just too many civilians. It's going to be the underground shopping center version of house-to-house fighting, I'm afraid."

"'Shopping center'?"

"There are about a hundred stores down there. Stay out of the deli in the front, by the escalators," Ari said "The prices are god-awful."

"Colmar, Boss," Rosie said. "Coming about."

"All right, everybody," Ari said, "rejoin your teams. One pass for me, as I said. Three stops for you and your teams. You've got thirty seconds each before I button up and go. After that, I'm going to take a run at that Terror Ship and see whether I can't disable it without killing all the kidnapped people inside. If I'm lucky, if it's where I think it is...we'll see. Good luck, all of you!"

They saluted and went out. Ari sat himself down, looking out. The cockpit windshield was a blur of charcoal-gray cloud. The Black Forest beneath them was lost in it, visible to radar but to nothing else. "How low are we?" Ari said to Rosie.

"Fifty feet above treetop, Boss. I'd rather not push it any further. Some of these trees get tall without warning."

"Don't push it on *my* account," Ari said. He strapped himself in at the gunnery console, wiped his hands on his uniform, and got himself settled. This one shot was going to matter profoundly. If that Battleship got up in the air again, he was going to have a lot more trouble than he wanted.

"Schaffhausen," Rosie said. "I'm starting descent. Increasing to two hundred knots."

Ari had to swallow. Even though they were less than forty feet above the streets of the small city, he couldn't even see the lights of the town, the fog was so thick. "Just be sure you don't hit anything pointy."

"No chance, Boss. I've got a nice, direct run-in. I'm running right down the S-bahn tracks, the local light rail. It's just like playing with slot cars."

It was beginning to feel like it, too. Rosie made a

rather abrupt left turn that would have knocked Ari out of his seat had he not been strapped in. He gulped and got busy with the gunnery console. This was one of the few problems he had in this business: letting someone else fly. It drove him crazy.

"Feeding heads-up to gunnery," Rosie said. Overlaying the green of the radar on the gunnery screen, the false-color images of the heads-up display now appeared. "Two minutes to primary target. I'll warn you at one. Passing the military airfield at Dübendorf." She listened to something in her earpiece. "They see us, but they're not doing anything."

It's all taken care of, said that cheerful voice in Ari's memory. Was this prearranged, he wondered. Or had someone in the government received a quick phone call from a UN PR office down in Andermatt, or from "the Hall of the Mountain King"? No telling now. No time to think about it.

Ari settled himself in the chair, did his best to become one with the gunnery screen. Odd, to be able to concentrate on shooting and not have to think about flying, as well—. That was the only good thing about this.

"One minute, boss. Acquisition."

Up over the "virtual horizon" of the gunnery screen came the image of the Katenberg on the right, the Zurichberg on the left, and between them the depression marking the old river delta of the Limmat, on which Zürich was built. At the end of it all lay the Zürichsee, Lake Zürich, stretching off in a long blob of residual heat, now that they were close enough to get a residual heat signature, as well. Closer, brighter, a smaller blob of light. Concentrated. Other signatures, as well: the presence of Elerium was registering.

Ari hunched himself over the joystick, ignoring the thought of what the "real world" looked like through the windshield at the moment. This was all that mattered, those slowly rising octagons emerging from what once was the Hauptbahnhof.

"Trouble, Boss!" Rosie said. "Getting some movement."

Ari swallowed. The Battleship had acquired their signal by now, he was very sure. He had hoped that approach from this side would win them a few precious seconds. Maybe it had. But the Battleship was moving, shouldering its way upward—though slowly. Very slowly.

Ari uncapped the fire button on the joystick. *Range isn't optimum,* he thought. *If I let loose with a fusion ball at this range, and I miss, the whole station and everybody in it'll—*

Plasma fire stitched the air all around them. Rosie did something sudden at her console, and the Avenger lurched upward and sideways through the air as she plunged toward the ruined train station. The ferocious lines of fire stitched along and upwards after them, the only thing visible through the fog. "Gonna drop her real quick, Boss," she said. "Three seconds—two—"

Fire or not? Hold it just for a second more— The bottom dropped out of the world. Ari swallowed and kept his eye on the screen, on his target. The Battleship was still rising, but not as fast as it should have. *What the hell—is it caught on something?* An infrared trace was showing, a faint network of residual heat, like a spiderweb tangled around the leftward end of the Battleship, and the rightward one, where the ship had sunk into the structure of the building—

Now, Ari thought, and fired.

There was always a moment after you hit the fire button, some X-COM people said, when the fusion-ball projector seemed to hold its breath and think about whether to blow up what you fired it at, or to blow *you* up. That moment came and went. A blur, a blob of light like a small sun, leapt away from the Avenger and struck the Battleship just right of its middle.

The night lit up, and everything around the half-destroyed train station showed clear in an actinic light like lightning for a long, long few seconds as the fusion ball did its work. Rosie veered east to miss the glare, then plunged on past the station, now visible (if nothing else was) through the fog. She had a look at it while Ari stared at his screen and tried to make sense of it.

"Half a minute to your first stop, Boss," she said. "Looks like you left some of that ship, but I don't think it'll be going anywhere soon. That stuff was all tangled around it—some kind of iron or steel reinforcement, I think. Meantime, the buildings around are still standing. Nice shooting."

"Super," Ari said. "Let's get the first team out. When we've dropped everybody, we'll go have a shot at that Terror Ship and see if we can't cripple it, too. Meanwhile, I'm going to go put on my armor." He undid the straps, got up, headed downstairs. "And then I'm going to get me a psi-amp and go hunting."

Four

ive hours later, the hunting was nearly over, though large parts of it had not gone according to anyone's expectations.

Jonelle met the remains of the first assault teams where the pilot of her Skyranger had dropped her, outside the Hauptbahnhof. She was in heavy armor, her flying suit—only sensible, since the area was not yet completely secured, and X-COM would take it most unkindly if a regional commander should be taken out by a chance shot from a Sectoid sniper. The use she would have preferred for the armor was to go down into the depths of the Hauptbahnhof and be busy in other ways. But she couldn't so indulge herself—not anymore, and particularly not now.

She met with Colonel Arnesson, who had been sent to Zürich after his interception team finished its work in the

Canaries. Together, with a couple of squaddies as *de facto* bodyguards, they walked down the Bahnhofstrasse, past the broken shop windows and the burned-out stores, and he briefed her.

"It seems as if the Battleship fell afoul of the cast-iron reinforcements in the old building," he said. "There was nothing like that in the new construction to give it any problems, but what it *did* sink through seems to have slowed it enough for Colonel Laurentz to stick the spear in its side, so to speak. When my team got in, we managed to get out about ninety civilians who were trapped in the ruble."

Jonelle nodded and looked around her. "How are they doing?"

"About eighty percent survival, the hospital says. Then the Avenger dropped its assault teams, just the other side of the river," Arnesson said. "The squads came across, destroyed the bridges, killed some Floaters they found on their way over, and started working northward. They met heavy resistance on the way up, and Colonel Laurentz broke off his attack on the Terror Ship down in Paradeplatz and flew down to help them. That's when the Avenger went down. The aliens had two teams with blaster launchers waiting down there. I suspect they were waiting for an attack from the south. If Ari had come in straight, he'd have been dead, and all his teams with him—not even an Avenger could have taken both those things in the teeth."

Jonelle nodded. Leaving strategic considerations aside,

Ari had a love of sneakiness for its own sake. He would never go straight when he could go crooked. Jonelle used to tease him, *Your brain could be used for a corkscrew, you know that?* And he would laugh.

"The Avenger went down just on the lakeside," Arnesson said, "into the water. That was what saved his and Melanchion's lives. They both got out OK—they were both armored, and Ari came out with a psi-amp. The crews say that to have heard Ari, as he went down, you'd have thought he was discussing what bus stop he was going to get off at, he was so casual. In the middle of ditching, he was still giving them instructions on how to attack the craft in Paradeplatz, and insisting on casualty reports."

"I wouldn't mind one of those myself," Jonelle said, a little tartly.

Arnesson looked at her in some surprise. "Weren't you given one already? My apologies, Commander—there's been a breakdown in communications somewhere. Of a total of thirty-four deployed, we lost ten."

"So many," she said softly.

"It's a miracle it wasn't more, Commander. We were spread very, very thin on the ground here, and if the aliens had had even a slight advantage in numbers or tactics, a whole lot more of us would be dead. As it was, our people fought like madmen...and the aliens, a lot of them, didn't seem to be functioning up to full efficiency after the Battleship went."

"The masterminds were on it," Jonelle said, "or at least so I suspect."

"Some of them, at least. We got several stunned Ethereals of several ranks off it, and various other dead ones. They've gone down to Irhil M'goun to be held until Doctor Trenchard gets back down there from 'Moria.'"

Jonelle smiled slightly. "Yes, he would want to be there for the interrogations. That's fine." She lost the smile, then, as they came to the Zürich branch of the F.A.O. Schwartz toy store. It was burned out, the biggest and most beautiful of the antique rocking horses in the front window lying on its side on a carpet of shattered glass, plasma burns marking its side. *He'll never buy me that horse now. Not that he could have anyway—the bloody thing costs about half a year's salary...and where would I have kept it?*

"At any rate, the initial teams' assaults were surprisingly successful, despite the aliens' resistance. We had a little unlooked-for help, too: a lot of the locals took exception to the terror raid and sniped at the aliens from their windows. Some of them died for their trouble...a lot of them did us some good. While the first-in teams were working north, Colonel Laurentz and his pilot made their way north as well, joining up with the southernmost team about twenty minutes into their attack. They were pushing north to join another team when they ran into an attack group of aliens apparently sent to stop them. That was where about a third of our casualties came, right there. There were two Ethereal leaders with the force, a lot of Snakemen, and some Chryssalids. The team killed the Chryssalids first, as you might expect, and then started working on the others. But they came under psi attack. According to the survivors, Colonel Laurentz engaged one of the Ethereals with his psi-amp and killed it—but the other one got control of several of his people and then forced them to attack him. There was a battle for control of their minds, apparently. Colonel Laurentz won it—just—but must have sustained some blow to his mind. He went down, and the teammates he had been protecting went down with him—a couple of them died. The others are on their way back to Irhil."

Jonelle nodded calmly. "And the colonel?" she said, as though no more concerned about him than about anyone else.

"After the fighting finished in this area, a recovery team made pickup on him and his teammates. He seems never to have regained consciousness after he went down, Commander. He was shipped down to Irhil with the rest of them. As far as I know, he's still comatose. I haven't heard any updates, though we should have one for you shortly."

"Very well. So. That particular alien attack was resolved, more or less in our favor, I take it. What happened to that other Ethereal?"

"It must have been considerably weakened by Colonel Laurentz's struggle with it, Commander. It was stunned and taken prisoner a little later, with surprisingly little trouble."

They stopped a block north of Paradeplatz, looking up at a shot-out window. Someone had draped a Swiss flag out of it at some stage of the fighting, and the flag lay limp and somewhat singed around the edges. "Around that time," Arnesson said, "my team came in. We put down troops and Heavy Weapons Platforms between the Limmat and the Sihl and began a sweep eastward to meet Colonel Laurentz's troops. The team from Greece landed at the train station and headed down inside.

"I'll want a more detailed report from them shortly," Jonelle said, "but what's the general story down there?"

"About six hundred civilians dead. A lot of Chryssalids and Zombies—we had to kill all those, of course. A whole lot of dead aliens of various kinds. At least eight of our own assault team members." Arnesson looked somber, and Jonelle guessed that some of those were his own people. "The station is in a bad way. Once we've got all the dead and wounded out of there, the place will probably have to be demolished."

"To think they just renovated it," Jonelle said. "Well, never mind. So the assault teams consolidated...."

"Yes, Commander. And several HWPs joined forces and began concentrating on the second alien craft, the Terror Ship. Colonel Laurentz was very insistent that we shoot the site up thoroughly."

"The site?" Jonelle said, looking at him curiously.

For the first time in all this, Arnesson, always something of a sobersides, cracked a small, thin smile. "You'd better have a look."

They walked on down the Bahnhofstrasse to the point where it bends slightly crossing Pelikanstrasse, and Jonelle gazed down at Paradeplatz, past the wreckage of burned and derailed trams—and opened her mouth, and shut it again.

The Terror Ship was tipped over on one end, sticking out of what appeared to be a large hole in the street. As they got closer, Jonelle could see that the upper levels of the hole were full of cables and conduits, and what appeared to be several hallways or corridors, some ten or fifteen feet under ground-level proper.

As they approached, they were joined by Mihaul O'Halloran, who came over to them and took off his helmet long enough to wipe some sweat out of his eyes. "Here's the colonel's catch of the day, Commander," he said. "The Battleship was nice shooting, but this one was just plain old wickedness in action. I'd give a pretty penny to know how he knew what was under here."

"What did he tell you, Mihaul?" Jonelle said as they walked over to the hole to examine it more closely.

"Not much, ma'am. He was crashing in the lake about that time, and after that, most of the way up here he was busy fighting. He couldn't give us detailed explanations. He just said to me, 'Do me a favor,' he says, 'see the ground all around that thing? Shoot it out.' And I said, 'What, Boss?' I mean, 'Sir.' Ma'am."

"Never mind, Mihaul."

"Yes, ma'am. Well, he said it again, 'Just do that. Get whatever firepower you can. Grenades, rocket launchers, heavy laser, I don't care. Concentrate on where the tracks are, first. Then just dig yourself a hole to China. Get some help. And you'll want to post a guard afterwards.'"

Mihaul shrugged. "So we did. It took the devil's own time to get anywhere with this. I mean, ma'am, we didn't see what point shooting at the ground was, anyway. And of course the aliens inside were shooting at us all the time. But after a little while, the ship started to sag over sideways—as if something under it were weakening. So we got two of those HWPs in as quick as we could, and let them really have a go at it. The ground gave way then, all right! Not just the ground, as you can see. And when it was over, the ship just fell right into the hole with almost all its weapons ports under the surface, and it couldn't shoot anything much after that but this underground stuff, nor go anywhere much after that but toward China. We had plenty of leisure to storm it then. We got out every single civilian that they'd stowed in it, without damaging it at all. Six captures, ma'am—Ron over there will give you the whole list. And," Mihaul said, and laughed softly, "we saw why the colonel said we might need to post a guard."

They came to the edge of the hole. The Terror Ship was tilted down into it at a forty-five degree angle, with God-knew-what alien lubricants spilling down from it, and water from broken pipes, and snapped wires and cables fizzing all around, so that everything stank of ozone and Lionel trains. And down there, under the ship, scattered higgledy-piggledy with corpses of Snakemen and Chryssalids, was the gold—the gold that lay in the sunken vaults all up and down the length of the

Bahnhofstrasse, vaults shared and policed by the Big Three banks, secret to most, known of in an abstract way by many, though this was not the kind of information that the Michelin guide normally reveals. There it lay, gold in heaps and piles, bars and bars of it, crushed and scattered under the remains of the Terror Ship, melted by the heat of all the weaponry concentrated on that spot since the attack that Ari ordered began—gold running away in little rivulets and puddling like bright coins, here and there still glowing red, most places just gleaming dully in wriggly, abstract sculptures and splashes on the sub-floor forty feet down.

Mihaul shook his head and laughed. "So we posted the guards, ma'am. Though I think anyone nuts enough to come *here* and try to steal probably deserves some."

"Mihaul," Jonelle said, "you're dead right. Well, the Swiss police will be along shortly to handle this. Meanwhile...let's go up to the station and see how they're doing."

All the way up, Jonelle received reports, asked questions and answered them, and started settling the dispositions of the teams once they'd gotten the Swiss started on the cleanup. She sent for a stripping team to start work on the Terror Ship—it would be a little while before the Battleship was ready to be stripped of all but the easiest things, such as the Elerium. *I'll have the funds for that new mind shield now,* Jonelle thought, *even a new hyperwave decoder.* That was possibly the brightest aspect of this whole situation. But all the time, as she gave orders and received information, Jonelle could not get rid of the memory of a night when she and Ari had been out on leave in Paris, and she had come back from shopping to find him exchanging terrible ethnic jokes with someone who (he later told her) was a genuine "Gnome" of Zürich, a junior manager with one of the Big Three banks, and who was full of interesting stories. Jonelle had afterwards laughed at the idea, and teased Ari for the better part of half an hour about how he so hated eating or drinking by himself that he'd strike up a conversation with anybody, even a banker.

And it was true. Oh, please, let it go on being true. Oh, Ari, please, don't die!

"So we have a mole," she said much later to DeLonghi, who looked at her out of a face pale with weariness, and now creased with shock.

"Here?"

"Possibly. Somewhere in the organization, certainly, or possibly among the Swiss. In any case, we have to look at who knows about the building of the new base, and start turning over some rocks to see what we find."

DeLonghi sighed. "Commander, with all due respect, I think we have more immediate problems. We're very shorthanded right now. Half our craft are down for maintenance of some kind. Several are seriously damaged and won't fly again before the end of the week, no matter how many engineering crew we put on the job—and we only have so many."

"I've requisitioned more," Jonelle said. "Some of the Andermatt staff will be coming down here."

"It's not going to be enough," DeLonghi said.

"Commander, if you're suggesting that we stop construction on the new base because we're having problems down here, I'm afraid that's not an option that's open to us—and senior command would laugh themselves blue if they heard it. After cashiering us, of course."

He looked more shocked than previously. "No, Commander, I didn't—"

"Good," Jonelle said.

"But we're still left materially unable to deal with any serious threat. We had an Interceptor destroyed, another one that's been seriously damaged and will be out of commission for about a week. One of our Skyrangers limped home on half its propulsion system—that one needs about a week in the shop, as well. One of our Lightnings was destroyed. One of the Firestorms that went out yesterday was damaged. The Avenger—" He shrugged. "That's worse—it's a write-off."

Jonelle smiled slightly. "That's what the insurance company says?"

DeLonghi threw a look at her that suggested he wasn't wild about the joke. "Commander," he said, "it's just a blessing that it was empty when it went down."

"It's not exactly a blessing," Jonelle said. "It has to do with Colonel Laurentz's disposition of the craft, I believe. He knew well enough that you don't keep an Avenger in the air with a full complement any longer than you have to. Which brings me to another subject."

DeLonghi swallowed. "What was he doing in that ship? My orders to him were most specific. He was not to put himself in the front line."

"Commander," DeLonghi said, with the air of a man who knows he's already beaten, "you know the situation last night. You've seen the transcripts and the timings. The colonel put a very compelling case to me. And your orders to me also required that I was to take his advice, unless I could find compelling reasons to the contrary. There were none. There were two large reasons sitting in Zürich, which meant when he said he was going, I had to let him. If the commander can suggest to me what she would have done in my place, in that situation—I'll listen gladly, and note the lesson for later."

Jonelle sat back and sighed. "Joe," she said, "sometimes you can be a real pain in the butt, you know that? But you've got me there. Well, all we can do is get on with requisitioning new supplies and equipment, and transferring in some new staff. At least we won't be short of money to pay for them."

"What was the total haul?" Jonelle shook her head. "I'm still working on the figures. But it's large. We've got a big Elerium supply now—I wouldn't exactly say we have it to burn, but we've got plenty on hand. I've ordered a mind shield and hyperwave decoder for the new facility. The first set of hangars are almost ready, and the living blocks. I want to move about half the engineering staff down there and start them making guns." She smiled, a slightly grim look. "We should do well up there. Some parts of Switzerland, you can't spit without hitting an arms dealer—the market's active enough for anybody."

"I'll take care of it tomorrow, Commander. Anything else?"

She shook her head. "I'll be going back to Andermatt tonight. My operations and command center was being installed today—I want to keep an eye on that, and see if I can hurry the hyperwave decoder, as well. That won't be in a minute too soon to please me."

"Operations down here, then...." DeLonghi trailed off.

She looked at him, knowing what he was asking: was she going to pull back command from him, after such a bad start? "Let's just say I'll be keeping a general eye on things. But otherwise, you're mistaken if you think I'm likely to have much time for you. We'll be salvaging the Avenger at the Andermatt site. Between that, and oversee-ing the new installations...." DeLonghi nodded. "There is one thing I want, though," Jonelle said. "I want an inven-tory of all communications activity in and out of Irhil over the last two weeks."

"All of it?"

"All. Including ship-to-ship. Not transcripts—just the basic records of who called who and when."

"Very well, Commander."

"Good. See to it."

She got up, went out, and walked down the corridor that led from her office to Operations and the rest of the base, greeting her people as she went. There were fewer of them than usual.

We have a traitor, she thought. *We have a spy in our ranks. Someone who may have been working with my people—friends with them—or seeming friends. But someone who has no trouble in, directly or indirectly, sending them to their deaths.* Jonelle sighed. She had sent people to their possible or probable deaths nearly every day lately—but it was a death she herself was willing to share if she had to. She had come close enough to that, in her own time as a team member. What she had great trouble understanding was how one of her own, or for that matter how anyone from Earth, could willingly sell information about Earth defenses to the aliens. Oh, Earth-based treason she could understand readily enough. Jonelle was enough of a student of military history to understand that, even as there are people who will readily sell weapons, any weapons, to any buyer—a tendency she was not above exploiting—there were other people who would as eagerly sell information, that deadliest of weapons, to whoever would buy, even the sworn enemies of the whole human race. But a traitor of one country against another could always just move to another country afterward. *Where do these people think they'll be able to escape to,* Jonelle thought, *when the aliens rule Earth and start making soup out of everything that walks? Do they think they'll move to the Moon? Don't they realize they're in the pot with the rest of us already?*

Apparently one of them didn't. Her feelings about such people were robust. If she caught any of them, she supposed she would have to submit them to due process and let them be tried. But if she caught any of them in the field, in the middle of a fight, she doubted she would be so upright. "Killed while trying to escape" was an old and effective excuse, behind which—especially in these times—the authorities tended not to look too closely. That suited her completely, especially since, in her view, whoever had fed the aliens the information about the change of command at Irhil M'Goun was directly responsible for the deaths of ten of her people.

Possibly eleven.

Jonelle made her way through the part of the living block that was set aside as the infirmary. It wasn't a large area—partly because of the typical space restrictions, partly because there was generally not much need for many beds. Most injuries suffered by troops out on ground assault were either severe enough to kill them right away, or minor enough—with the present medical technology—to see them either ambulatory, or able to recuperate in quarters or ship out to a real hospital, within several days or a week. Some few cases, though, fell outside these boundaries.

There were two doctors who usually manned the place. Pierre Fleurie was off duty today. Jonelle found Gyorgi Makharov on duty instead. He was sitting at his desk by the corridor door, scribbling frantically on someone's chart as she came in.

He looked up at her out of those startlingly blue eyes of his, and frowned. In his young face, the expression made him look a little like a pouting child. Jonelle tensed a little. She had quickly learned that that frown on Gyorgi meant all was not well with the world—and, specifically, with his patients.

"Commander," he said. "They've been keeping you busy...."

"They have been, Gyorg," she said. "How is he?"

"Not conscious yet."

"What happened to him?"

"Psychocortical shock," Gyorgi said, pushing the chart away with a disgusted look. "The usual."

Jonelle nodded; the syndrome was all too familiar. It had come as a surprise, the first time people started running up against Ethereals and the other psi-talented species of aliens, that there was actual physical damage to the brain associated with psychic attack. It seemed that the brain interpreted attack "from within" as physical, at the chemical level—a finding that, paradoxically, had sped up X-COM's researches into the adaptation for humans of the technology that would eventually become the psi-amp. The problem was that, because the injury to the brain was literally a psychosomatic one, it didn't respond to the treatments that would normally have been useful for straightforward brain damage. Often enough, brains that seemed very little damaged did not survive, leaving a body that might function well enough, but that had no one "at home" in it, and was good for nothing but transplant parts. Others, who took more massive and physical-seeming damage, made more or less full recoveries. It was a puzzling part of neurophysiology, unpredictable and frustrating—so her medical staff had told Jonelle, more than once. More than once she had bugged them about coma cases whose etiology she couldn't understand. This one was going to be no exception.

"Can I see him?"

"Sure. By the way," Gyorgi added as she went past him toward the infirmary's bed wing, "he also took a good knock on the head, either when he fell or just before. He had a case of *contrecoup* when he came in that I thought might kill him all by itself—but it's reduced nicely without surgery, and there was no significant damage to the brain."

"*Contrecoup*?"

"You hit somebody on one side of the head," Gyorgi said, "and the bruise forms on the inside of the other side—the brain actually slams up against the bone. Fortunately"—and he looked somewhat wry—"the colonel either has softer bone or a harder brain than most people. He broke some minor blood vessels on the inside surface of the *pia mater*, but that was all. His other problems are worse."

Jonelle nodded and went on back.

There were only four beds in the wing, two of them screened off. The first one had a squaddie named Molson in it. Jonelle stopped, looked at the chart hung over the records rack at the bottom of the bed.

"Molson?" she said. "How you doing?"

"OK, Commander. A little chopped up, is all."

"Is it OK to look?"

"If you don't feel like throwing up—"

She put her head through the curtain. Molson was lying there with one leg up in traction, sandbags on either side of his body, and a cervical collar and "crown brace" around his skull, fastened by steel pins inserted through the skin and into the bone. Jonelle suspected this was no time for bothering with a bedside manner, especially when the voice that answered her had been relatively cheerful. "Good God, man," she said, "you look like the Bride of Frankenstein."

"Pinhead, my buddy Rogers says."

"That too. They're going to ship you up to the main hospital shortly, I take it."

"In a couple of days, yeah. Doc says 'after I stabilize.' Jeez, Commander, I've got enough metalwork stuck in me to stabilize anything."

"Well, you get your beauty sleep, Molson." She gave him a wicked look. "I'd say you could use it."

"Thanks loads, Commander." His eyes flickered toward the next bed over. "How's he doing—the colonel?"

"Catching up on his beauty sleep too, or so I hear," Jonelle said. "If we had anything around here so low-tech as a baseball bat, I'd take it to the big lazy lump."

"Yeah, well, give him one for me," Molson said. "He saved my butt last night."

"I'll do that."

She let the curtain fall and stepped over to the other bed, where the curtain was only partially drawn.

He was lying on his side in a position that immediately looked wrong in Jonelle's eyes. Whenever Ari lay on his side, he always curled up like an infant—something

Jonelle had teased him about more than once. Now he lay stretched out, one arm tucked under, one laid over the covers, in a position she recognized as part of the usual turning routine used on comatose patients. In a little while Gyorgi would come in and turn Ari onto his back, or his front. She was determined not to be there for that. The sight of this strong, lithe body flopping helpless and limp, like a doll, would do bad things for her composure.

There was no chair by the bed. She had to stand and look down on him, his unruly blond hair somewhat lank at the moment, for with other more pressing medical matters to attend to, no one would have washed it. That hurt her as much, in its way, as his odd position, for Ari was always personally fastidious. She had accused him once of taking more baths than a cat, and he'd laughed and said, "There's enough dirt in the world—I don't want any of it sticking to me."

His face was untroubled. He might have been sleeping, except that his breathing was so quick that it sounded slightly unhealthy. *Amazing,* Jonelle thought, *how much you can come to notice about a person, even about how they are just when they're sleeping. Let alone about the things they say, they do....* She looked down at that amiably ugly face, so very still when it was usually so mobile. Even in sleep, it would twitch, expressions coming and going in flickers that surfaced from his dreams.

Jonelle breathed out. "This is a very untenable position, Colonel," she said. "A bad spot. You get your butt out of that bed. I need your help—and your teams need you."

She stood quiet for a few breaths, and then—with a

reminder to herself that the next bed was occupied—began giving Ari a briefing, as she would have were he awake: how the raid went, the success of his stratagem in Zürich, who was alive. She didn't mention who was dead. When she finished, Jonelle said, "I have to go back to Andermatt. If you need me, just ask. Gyorgi will keep me posted on how you're doing."

She reached down and touched his face. "Take care of yourself, my lion," Jonelle said, very softly, not for the ears in the next bed to hear. Then she turned and left, keeping her voice cheerful and matter-of-fact as she said good night to Molson in the next bed, and to Gyorgi as she went out into the hall. It was all just part of the job, after all. It was the commander's business to keep up hope for everybody else, even when she wasn't sure where to find it for herself.

The next morning, Jonelle was back up under the mountain, inspecting the progress there. The living quarters were nearly finished: the last of the cooking facilities were going in as she made her tour. Work on the alien containment facilities was still ongoing. There were some details Jonelle had wanted added, some extra security doors and so forth. For her money, you could never be too careful about aliens when they were inside your own base. The first hangar space was within hours of being complete.

That morning, after much thought, she had told DeLonghi that she was taking the Skyranger that was presently doing transport duty between Andermatt and Irhil, and would be moving it permanently into Andermatt that afternoon, along with its crew and a small maintenance team for it. She was also taking two Lightnings.

He argued bitterly with her about this, but lacking better reasons—for she had none, only a growing streak of what she hoped was healthy paranoia—she finally had to fall back on good old-fashioned rank-pulling. She explained to him that this was just the way it was going to be. They did not part company on warm terms, which Jonelle regretted but was perfectly willing to cope with. She too had occasionally had to cope with disagreements with a superior officer, and there was no regulation that said one had to like it—just to comply.

Jonelle spent the better part of that day seeing that the new hangar space was to her liking. By and large, it was—large being the operant term. The most finicky bit of business had been the removal of the old steam catapult, neither the Skyranger nor the Lightnings needing anything of the kind. But while she checked the work of the hangar teams, other issues were on Jonelle's mind. If someone was indeed getting intelligence from inside her base about the battle-readiness of Irhil M'Goun, or its lack of it, she intended to find out quickly. This was another of the reasons DeLonghi had been unhappy.

"Let's see," Jonelle had said, "just how good their intelligence is. I'm going to go down to our hangars, notify the pilots myself, put them in their craft and send them off. No one else is to know where they're going, not even our own air traffic control. We'll be credited shortly for the various consumables we picked up during the Battleship capture. I'll have the Lightnings I'm taking replaced within the week. That information, too, is to stay between you and me. When the new ones are ready, they're going to be delivered to me at Andermatt, under wraps, and the old ones will be 'returned' to you down here."

And so it had been arranged. The completion of the living-quarters work being literally about as interesting as watching paint dry, Jonelle divided her attention for the rest of the day between the installation of the new control and command center—all modular and meant to "plug and play," a smart development in situations where fast replacement was vital, such as after a base attack—and watching the drying of another batch of paint: the markings on the vast number-one hangar floor. Space for one Avenger was marked out, for one Skyranger, two Lightnings, and two Interceptors. There was room for much more hardware downstairs on the number-two and number-three hangar levels, but it would be weeks yet before those were ready. Off to the sides of the huge, hollowed-out space was room for the Heavy Weapons Platforms and other ancillary gear—weapons lockers and the smaller ammunition storage "pots."

She watched with satisfaction as the first of the Lightnings came in, in mid-afternoon, and settled into the spot prepared for it. The entrance had been adapted with a set of camouflaged sliding doors that looked, from outside the mountain, like a stony cornice overhung with snow.

Unfortunately, the snow that gathered above it, also part of the camouflage, had a tendency to fall in through the opening doors, shortly thereafter leaving the floor awash in meltwater, and the markings teams began complaining about what it was probably doing to their incompletely dried paint job.

When they started yelling about this for the second time, on the arrival of the second Lightning, Jonelle realized it was time to get out of there. She went down to her quarters—a very bare-bones arrangement so far, barely more than a camp bed with a desk off to one side, on which was mounted her terminal to the command-and-control network installation—and went rooting around in her closet for the necessary civvies for going to town.

This, of course, was no simple matter. It meant first checking the train schedule to make sure that the way would be clear for the little automated shuttle car. After going to all this trouble over the new base, there would be no point in being killed by the 4:10 Inter-City from Göschenen to Basel. Once you'd checked, you then went down in the elevator, called the car with the control in the elevator, put on a big, loose coverall (which wrought havoc with your skirt, if you were wearing one) and a fluorescent reflective vest so that at first glance you looked like railway personnel. Then you waited on the chilly, windy platform—an amazing forty-mile-an-hour draft came through that tunnel at all times—until the car came along and stopped for you. Once on it, you activated the controls that started it trundling back up to the light at the end of the tunnel. There it veered off to one side, onto an auxiliary track before and to one side of the main Göschenen station platforms. The track ran through what was essentially a little shed open at both ends. You climbed out, hung up your railway gear neatly on a hook provided for the purpose, and then made your way down a flight of stairs inside the "shed," through an underground passage and out through a plain locked door, which let you into the other underground corridors, which more normal passengers changing trains at Göschenen used to get from one track to another. After that, you walked around the end of the main-line platforms to the smaller one, which serviced the little "slanted" Göschenen-Andermatt train. You climbed aboard, showed the conductor your rail pass, and waited a few minutes until the little train hooted and started on its winding, leaning way up through the Schöllenen Gorge.

At the little station at Andermatt, you would get off to find yourself surrounded by either mad skiers waiting for one of the local commuter trains to take them up to the ski-drag lines at the bottom of the Oberalp Pass, or else a crowd of sated tourists, some rather the worse for wine drunk at unusual altitude, just off the Glacier Express, breaking the seven-hour trip before continuing on to either St. Moritz or Zermatt. Jonelle found herself among the skiers this time, it being a little late in the day for the tourists.

She made her way to the turnstile through what, as far as she could tell, was an impassioned argument about ski wax among a batch of fluorescently clad downhill enthusiasts. Out she went into the station parking lot, then full (in the swiftly falling dusk) of the cars of parents meeting kids now returning from the senior school in the next town over, Hospental. Once past the cars, Jonelle turned right at the bottom of the parking lot, past the tourist board building, and walked a little down the main street until the gap in the wall where she could cut through the town's park to the center of Andermatt village proper.

With the snow beginning to fall again through a dusk going peach-colored from sunset light coming from a rift in clouds to the west, and the lights coming on warm in stores and houses, the town was an inviting place. There was very little architecture in Andermatt that was modern-looking. Most houses and buildings were wooden, either new wood, beautifully golden, or old wood, sometimes a couple of hundred years old, aged to a brown so dark it was almost black. And the architecture was generally a lot alike—broad, flat, shallowly sloping Alpine roofs, sometimes with stones on top to hold the tiles on (though once, on one of the local restaurants near a ski slope, Jonelle discovered that what she thought were stones were actually potatoes destined for *rosti*, and put up there in the snow to cool faster after boiling). Those buildings that were stuccoed rather than wooden were usually decorated with *sgraffito*, the swirling, abstract designs cut through white plaster into a deeper, gray plaster layer. The whole place was almost offensively rustic, quiet, and pretty, and (inevitably for Switzerland) clean.

Jonelle heartily wished she had some time to spend

here that was not going to be taken up with concerns about traitors, equipment shortages, and other, deeper troubles. But since there was no chance of that, at least in the foreseeable future, she enjoyed the few minutes she had to spare, crunching through the foot-deep snow in the park. The quiet was pleasant, after the echoing clangor of the Hall of the Mountain King. There was little sound anywhere except the soft rush of the occasional car going by on the main road, the subdued jingle of snow chains, and the distance-muted shouts of children pelting one another with snow-balls over by the west side of the park, near the residential part of town.

She came out into the middle of town by the small alley that led past the town hall and made her way down to the "UN" office. Her PR assistant, an earnest young squaddie named Callie Specht, was tidying away the contents of her desk into a locked filing cabinet. She stood up hurriedly at the sight of Jonelle and said, "Oh, C—Ms. Barrett, I mean—"

"Hi, Callie," Jonelle said, and shrugged out of her jacket. "Busy day?" Specht nodded. "Anything interesting?"

"No, ma'am. The usual complaints about the interference of government—their government and all the others—and about people from the army stomping around, doing God knows what—"

"They mean us?"

"No," Callie said, "I think they really do mean their army. This town may depend on it for a lot of its income, but they're still ambivalent about it. And a lot more about cows..."

Jonelle chuckled. "Inevitable. Listen: you go on ahead. Leave me the keys—I'll lock up here."

Her squaddie went on willingly enough. Jonelle locked herself in and lost herself, for half an hour or so, in the business of finishing cleaning the place up for the night while her head buzzed with figures and conjectures.

Now that the number-one hangar is ready—and I've got my Lightnings out of harm's way—what next? The mind shield, or the hyperwave decoder? Which first? If they can have the containment area ready by the end of the week, I'd say the mind shield.

She went over it and over it. There were arguments for both pieces of equipment, but none of them seemed so overwhelming that it would leave her with a clear answer. Jonelle suspected that this was either because there really was not much difference between the two at the moment, or because she was dead tired and in no condition to make a choice on which lives might depend. *Probably the latter.*

She looked around her, could see nothing else that needed doing, and got busy securing the office. As she was locking the front door, a crowd of cheerful men in cold weather gear were heading up the street toward her, most of them familiar faces that she had seen in the office over the past week. One of them was Ueli Trager, the president of the town. The men were laughing and joking, and one of them was waving a wad of cash in another one's face.

The president saw Jonelle standing there and paused while his crowd of cronies went on ahead. "Fräulein Barrett!"

he said. "If you are done for the day, perhaps you will come and celebrate with us?"

"What's the occasion?"

"My cow," Trager said, "has gone into the national qualifiers."

"Forgive me," Jonelle said, somewhat bemused, "but I seem to have missed something. The national qualifiers for what?"

"The *stierkampf*, the *pugnieradienst*," the president said, "the cow fights which determine the herd leaders for the next year."

"Well, congratulations! I'm sure—" Jonelle stopped, slightly embarrassed. "I'm sorry—I've forgotten her name. And after you told me, the other day."

"Fräulein," Trager said, looking at her with a surprised expression, "it's very kind of you even to be concerned about such a thing. At any rate, my Rosselana"—and he broke into a grin broader than Jonelle had ever seen on anyone there—"has, I think the English idiom would be 'cleaned up.' We are going down to the Krone to celebrate. Come on along!"

From these fairly reserved people, Jonelle felt sure that such an invitation was rare. *Besides, it would be good PR. And it's not like I couldn't use something else to think about at the moment.* "Well, thank you," she said. "I think I will."

She found, as she and Trager rejoined his friends and they made their way to the hotel, that reserve was not on any of their minds. They did not go to the Krone directly—they went right down to the main street, to where it curved and the other biggish hotel sat, the Stern und Post. From outside it, where some townspeople had been sitting and drinking, they collected about another ten men and women and then doubled back up to the Krone again, laughing and shouting all the way. Jonelle wondered how they were going to fit into the bar there—and indeed they didn't. That bar was about twice the size of her office back in Irhil M'Goun, no more. But somehow, in the next ten or fifteen minutes, there were about ten or fifteen people packed into that little space, shoulder to shoulder, all very determinedly drinking schnapps and paying off a lot of bets.

Jonelle ordered a glass of the local white wine, and as she watched several particularly large cash transactions take place, she said to Ueli, only partly in jest, "Goodness, I didn't know this kind of thing played such an important part in your local economy!"

Ueli grinned and waggled his eyebrows at her. "It is strictly seasonal."

"But there seems to be a lot of interest. Some of these gentlemen have been collecting other people's bets, it seems—"

"Well, lots of people in town either work with the herds routinely, or own cows themselves, or have friends who work with the herds or own cows.... A lot of competitive feeling builds up."

"What amazes me," Jonelle said, "is that the cows remember who wins these contests when they go out to pasture again in the spring. They *do* remember?"

"Oh, yes indeed. They're not stupid. They have better memories than you might suspect—these cows in particular. They have been bred away from the original stock some-what—what Americans call the 'Brown Swiss.' But they are the culmination of a long selective breeding program. Down here, where the population is so sparse and some-times we cannot spare people to be with the cows all the time, especially at busy times like the spring and fall, the cows have to learn to take care of themselves. They have been bred to do so. And the *pugnieras*, the fighting cows, are bred to take care of the others, as well. It is a very special blend of aggression and caution, in these cows. I don't think there would be any question that they are smarter than usual. Not to mention more hardy, and more active—almost athletic, you might say."

Something clicked in Jonelle's mind, and she found herself thinking about the increase in cow stealings and mutilations down this way. *I wonder... who besides humans might be interested in the genetic heritage of cows that are so different from the norm? One more thing to look into....* "So when does she compete again, your cow? Maybe I should put some money down."

Ueli nodded at her, an approving look. "Well," he said, "in all honesty, you must know what to bet on. Peter? Peter, lean over this way, this lady is looking to bet in the nationals...."

Much more drinking followed, and much more discus-sion of the best points of a fighting cow: big shoulders, a deep chest, short horns rather than long ones—though this particular characteristic was argued with great passion from several sides. An hour or so later, Jonelle knew more than she ever needed to on the subject. Around then, the conversation began to trail off and was replaced by singing. They sang like angels, these people. One of the biggest and brawniest-looking of the men, whom Jonelle had first thought was a farmer (only to find that he ran one of the ski lifts on the north side of town), was producing an astonishingly high, pure, sweet soprano, while the others followed him in tenor and bass harmony, about twenty strong, in some mournful piece of local folk music. It was deafening, and made Jonelle's head pound somewhat...or was that the wine?

She made her excuses, thanked Ueli, and headed out into the night. There she shivered—the cold was beginning to get to her again. It was snowing again, through still air. She walked back to the train station, caught the slanty train down to Göschenen, and called the little rail car to take her back up to the Hall of the Mountain King. She had some phone calls to make.

By the end of the evening, the data-processing centers at four other X-COM bases were sick of the sound of her voice. She refused to leave them alone until they gave her figures on cattle heists and mutilations, which at the moment the other bases seemed to consider a lot less important than the human abductions presently going on. But Jonelle pressed. When she was finished, she had more data than she was quite sure what to do with, so she began attacking it in the simplest way: by having a spare map of the world printed out for her, so that she could begin sticking pins in it.

Late that night she heard the scream of engines from upstairs and went up to see a Skyranger arrive, along with the second group of maintenance crew and extra pilots. Enough of the living block was ready to put them up, and she showed them down there herself and got them settled, warning that service in the cafeteria was likely to be spotty until the rest of the venting was installed for the catering ranges. They took it cheerfully enough, which Jonelle could understand: pilots were notorious for having extra food cached in their quarters, just in case. "The *really* important question," one of them called after her when she left them to get settled, "is where's the Crud table?"

She laughed as she made her way back to her own quarters. The desk terminal, her link to the command-and-control center, showed no messages waiting. Jonelle looked at it, reached out to it, stopped herself, and then went ahead and touched the button to call Comms. "Anything from Irhil for me?" she said.

"No, Commander," came the Comms officer's voice. "Are you turning in now?"

"Yes."

"Do you want me to call you if I hear anything?"

"Yes, please."

Wearily, Jonelle locked up, undressed, and got into bed. Her mind was buzzing with cows and hyperwave decoders. Business...she could have been grateful for it, except that it didn't do what it should have done. It didn't shut out the one thought that wouldn't go away. The still face on the pillow, the body stretched out sideways, not curled up properly, the concern that, in the proper conduct of her duty, she must put aside during the day—and with which she was now alone, in the dark.

When it went off, the alarm on the console sounded about a hundred times more jarring than she had expected it would—the acoustical brightness of this little bare-walled room with nothing on the walls. Her mind cried, *Ari!* She fumbled for the lamp, found it, stumbled out of bed toward the console, and slapped the comms button. "Yeah?"

"Trouble, Commander. M'Goun's got a hot one coming our way."

"What are they sending?"

"Nothing, Boss. They're empty."

"What, again? Shit! Can't anyone else—"

"No, Commander. That's why they called."

"Scramble the pilots and an assault team," she said, heading for the closet to get dressed. "We're going. What have they picked up?"

"Large Scout, ma'am."

"Right. That means one of the Lightnings, and have the Skyranger loaded as backup. Get them moving."

She pulled out a flight coverall, scrambled into it, pulled on her boots. *Thank God the pilots are here*, she thought. *I sure couldn't fly, not six hours after drinking.* Jonelle went pounding out the door into the screech and hoot of the newly installed Klaxons. As she went by one installation, she noticed one hooter that wasn't working. *Make a note of that—*

Up the stairs. The place was coming quickly alive. The bright lights were on in the number-one hangar, pilots and crews already hurrying out into the big space. Some of them looked at Jonelle in astonishment as she headed for the equipment rack and pulled off her flying armor. "Ma'am—" one of them said.

It was a captain, her only one, Matthews. She wheeled on him. "We've got nobody higher-ranked on hand than you right now, Matt. I will not send out a ground assault with no one higher-ranking to advise. That's me. Get your team suited and get them loaded!"

People ran in all directions. "Command," Jonelle shouted, "where are they?"

"Over Bellinzona now, Boss," the voice came back. "Heading northeast."

Chur, she thought. That was the first city of any size nearby. Thirty thousand people—the aliens would have a party there, if allowed to land. "I don't want them to get any farther north than our latitude," she yelled to Comms and the public at large. "Let's go!"

The Skyranger's troop complement was loading; its HWP was getting ready to trundle into position, last in to be first out. Jonelle headed for the Lightning. As she did, the new hangar exit door slid open. Snow fell inside in a great lump and splatted wetly on the floor. "I've got to do something about that," she muttered as she ducked through the Lightning's door.

She made her way up to the ship's cockpit, buttoned up, and started to lift. There was barely room for her to wedge herself into the observer's seat behind the young pilot, Ron Moore.

"Ronnie," she said, "all we've got on this one are Stingray missiles. Your job isn't to get too close to that guy. Just hurt him, put him down as fast as you can. But under no circumstances are you to let him get any farther north than Andermatt."

"You got it, ma'am." Ron hit his comms control to put his chat with Central Command at Irhil M'Goun on "open air." "Central, where's our baby?"

"Transferring our targeting to you until you acquire," said Central. The screens in the cockpit came alive as the Lightning shot out the opened door in the mountain, and Jonelle braced herself in place—no straps would fit around the flying suit.

"Thanks, Central, we'll need it. Cloud's bad. Ceiling eighteen and snow."

Gray cloud boiled against the cockpit windows. "He's still heading northeast," Ron said. "Four thousand meters."

"Wouldn't go much lower than that if I were him," Jonelle muttered. In this neighborhood, the higher mountaintops could come up on you with deceptive speed.

"Neither would I, ma'am," Ron said. "Still heading northeast. I think he wants to go to ground in the Lukmanier Pass."

"Don't let him in there," Jonelle said. "He'll run right up to the main east-west valley and have a straight shot at Chur. Waste a shot or two if you have to, but turn him, Ronnie."

"Will do, Boss," the pilot said.

He climbed, heading southeast to intercept. Conventional motion detection picked the alien up as they were swinging past the peak of Piz Paradis, one of the taller mountains southeast of Andermatt. "There he is," said Ron, and the screen lit with the trace of the large Scout ahead of them.

"Force him up—don't let him down into the valley!"

"Stingray one," said Ron, "targeting—"

At this range? Jonelle thought, but even with as big a miss as Ron was likely to make, the Scout might still turn at the shot across its bow. This part of the chase was going to be up to Ron, at any rate.

"Stingray one away—"

The Lightning gave the little idiosyncratic jump, which was typical when it launched a missile. Jonelle peered at the radar and motion detection screens, which were more than usually difficult to read, cluttered with ground artifact from the mountainous terrain below. The alien craft was shooting straight as an arrow for Chur: northeast, northeast—and then abruptly, it zagged almost due westward.

"He's out of the valley, Boss. Heading toward Sedrun, right into the mountains now."

"Good. Put him down as deep in as you can. I don't want him near anybody."

They plunged through the air over the mountains, passing over the small town of Sumvitg, south of the main east-west valley. "Some nice glaciers down there, Boss," Ron said, comparing the heads-up display's map against the radar/motion detection screen. "Wouldn't bother anybody if we knocked him down there, would it?"

"Only us," Jonelle said, shivering, "on recovery. You really want to do a ground assault on a glacier?...But if it seems the best spot, never mind, just do it!"

She watched the screen. They were creeping closer to the Scout. "Thirty kilometers now," said Ronnie. Then a few moments passed. "Twenty-five...Stingray two targeting. Acquire. Launch!"

The Lightning bounded again. A third dot appeared, the missile. Jonelle watched the targeting trace from the missile lock onto the alien craft, watched the two dots draw closer together, closer, almost merge—

The alien craft jogged sideways again, southward, just as the missile should have struck it. Ron swore. "Sorry, Boss," he said. "Still too much range. And they know the speed of these missiles too well—I wish I had some more vector to add. I'm closing—"

The Lightning leapt after the Scout. The Scout leapt too, almost due southward now. "Whatever he's going for," Ron said, "it won't be Chur, not unless he does another one-eighty."

"He may have that in mind. You just make sure you put one of these up his butt before he gets a chance, Ronnie."

"Kinky," Ron said mildly. The Lightning accelerated— Jonelle had to brace herself more firmly.

"Don't let him get as far south as the San Bernardino pass," Jonelle said. "He'll vanish down that like water down a drain."

"I won't," Ron said. "Twenty kilometers now, Boss. Targeting Stingray three now. Acquire—"

"Wait for fifteen kilometers, Ron—"

"That's my intention, ma'am."

She watched as the two dots, the Scout and the Lightning, slowly slid closer together. "Fifteen point four—fifteen point two. Fifteen kilometers—firing!"

Bound! went the Lightning. Once again a third dot appeared as the missile leapt away. The targeting trace from the missile indicated positive lock. They watched while the dots inched closer, closer, merged—

The screen flashed. "It's a hit!" Ron said, but the Scout didn't slow or veer. "Damn. Not enough damage. Must have winged him."

"Once more," Jonelle said softly.

"Loading four—he's still heading south. Nope," Ron added. "Angling west, now."

Deeper still into more remote territory, Jonelle thought. If that Scout knew where they had come from, it was definitely trying to get them as far away from any kind of help as possible. "It had better be the next one, Ronnie," Jonelle said, "or you won't have anything to protect us with if a friend of his shows up. And if he gets much farther south, and you drop him there, he's going to fall right on St. Moritz. That would *not* be a good thing."

Ron looked furious. "Four ready," he said. "Accelerating. Ten kilometers. If I can't hit him at that range, Boss—"

Jonelle said nothing. Ron's face set. "Targeting. Acquire. Firing!"

The fourth missile leapt away. They watched. Jonelle clenched her teeth, thinking, *Come on, you, come on!* The dots drew closer, drew closer. Merged. The screen flashed—

"It's a hit!" Ron cried, and the forward speed of the dot representing the alien Scout decreased abruptly. It veered almost due south. "Going down, Boss! Tracking now. Losing altitude: one thousand meters—five hundred—passing over the lake—now gaining a little. He's trying to make it over the mountain—" Ron chuckled.

The dot stopped. "Down," Ron said. "On the north slope of...what's its name here? Monte dell'Oro. One of the mountains south of the lake."

Jonelle bit her lip. It was not the kind of place she would normally choose for a ground assault. Attacking either uphill or downhill was a nuisance, no matter what the tacticians said. You wound up with gravity as the chief enemy, in a fight where you already had one that was deadly enough. But this was no time to be complaining. "Right. Notify the Skyranger that our boy's on the ground, and then take us down easy. Nice shooting, Ronnie!"

She turned and went back to talk to her people, a last few words before they put their tender skins out where aliens could shoot at them. In her own days as sergeant and captain and colonel, Jonelle had always made sure to take those few moments, for the simple reason that— ground assaults being what they were—it was likely to be your last chance to ever talk to some of these people. Or, alternately, their last chance to talk to *you*. But what she mostly wanted to communicate to them now was something she had been feeling on and off since she left Ari's bedside:

I'm sick of sitting around. I'm going to go kill *something.*

* * *

The Lightning grounded, harder than necessary per-haps—a function of the bad terrain, or of the fact that Ron Moore was better at flying than he was at landing. Jonelle hefted her heavy laser and said, "Everybody ready, now?"

From the others, all armored, came a chorus of "Yes, Boss" and "Let's go!"

The Lightning's deployment doors opened out over the icy ground strewn with rocks and boulders. It helped a little that the Lightning's jets had blown the site mostly clear of snow, but around the Scout there was still a fair amount, and the wind whipping past them was bringing more in the beginnings of drifts from the upper slopes of the neighboring mountain. At least there was no danger of an avalanche: all the snow that could fall down in the immediate neighborhood *had* fallen down.

Fire erupted from the downed Scout. It might not be able to fly, but at least some of whatever aliens were in-side it were apparently all right. This annoyed Jonelle, and made her suspect that the inmates were of the more robust types of aliens. *Damn.*

"By fours," she said to the sergeant in the other team. "Don't hurry. Get your folks safely disposed, and if there's snow for them to use as cover, have them make the most of it. It's no protection, but it can be a distraction."

Jonelle's first four went out, one of them with a mo-tion scanner.

"Nobody outside, Boss," said the squaddie with the motion detector after a few moments. "Nobody out here at all but us chickens—whoops! Six high!"

Something moved upslope, on the narrow ledge at the top of a jagged cliff face. Squaddies whirled, fired. The creature leapt apart in a burst of blood, shrieked, and fell down among them.

They all stared. It looked like a goat, but it was bigger, and had huge back-curved horns. "Holy shit," one of the squaddies said. "It's a big-horn sheep."

"It's an ibex," someone else said.

Jonelle shook her head regretfully. "It's *toast*," she said. "Poor thing. Never mind. It's getting on toward breakfast time—let's go crack this egg." She hefted her laser cannon and left the Lightning, followed by three more of her squad.

The assault took the better part of two hours. From Jonelle's point of view, it was the usual crazed, confused melange of noises, images, and general craziness, every-thing seeming to happen at once. Afterward, people always told Jonelle how organized and cool she seemed, and how structured her handling of the situation was. She never believed it. She always lost track of how many grenades she had thrown, how many targets she had fired at, lost, fired at again. Her heavy laser was damaged about halfway through the assault, and she was forced to pick up one belonging to one of her dead squaddies and work with that—something that always obscurely both-ered Jonelle when she was fighting. She thought of the life this weapon should have saved, and didn't, through lack of skill or bad luck—there was never any way to tell, and it was too late now. She fired at and killed every alien that came within sight of her, first assessing them for com-mercial value, but all of them seemed strangely devalued today. One she stunned, a Snakeman leader who would at least be useful for interrogation. Her team did most of the aliens in before she had a chance. She wondered whether the cold was slowing her down, or whether her people were simply actively protecting her. There was no telling. She wished they would concentrate more on themselves. For herself, she went on firing.

By the time the shooting stopped, four of her people were dead inside that ship, or outside, in the dark, in the drifting snow. Jonelle and the survivors, including the sergeant, stood around shortly thereafter, surveying the wreckage of the ship. "Kind of strange, if you ask me, Boss," said the sergeant.

Jonelle was still trying to make sense of it. "How many of them did you say?"

"Four Snakemen, including the leader. Two Chryssalids and a whole pile of Silacoids."

"Silacoids," Jonelle muttered, shaking her head. "Why?"

"Seven of them," said one of the squaddies, rejoining the group. "I just got the last one—it was trying to run away in the snow. They don't do too well at that—the snow melts off them, and the trails are kind of obvious, they're so hot."

"All right," Jonelle said. "Let's clean up here. Strip the ship of things that can be easily carried, and make pickup on the corpses. Get the prisoners stowed. I'll call Irhil for a strip team to get the metal and the other consumables."

She made her way slowly back to the Lightning. That was when the last Chryssalid jumped her. The thing seized her with its claws, hunting for somewhere to inject the venom that would put out her humanity like a candle being snuffed. Jonelle grappled with the thing, gasping with revulsion. After a moment her suit training cut in, and she jumped, and flew. There she hung, in midair, badly balanced and wondering if she was going to crash—hovering, or trying to, in a storm of blowing snow, while the Chryssalid hung from her, squirming and shrieking and thrashing, trying to breach her armor.

Both her hands were busy holding it away. Jonelle had nothing to get a shot at it with, and her people wouldn't dare shoot at it for fear of hurting her. As if this wasn't enough, a gust of wind blew her, back first, into the nearby cliff face from which the poor ibex had been blasted.

OK, Jonelle thought. *Two can play at that game.* She forced the suit to leap back away from the cliff again, and swung herself around in midair, so that the Chryssalid was toward the wall of stone. Then she launched herself at the cliff, full force.

Some time before, back in the States, Jonelle had gone with some friends from the Washington base to a crab joint near the Inner Harbor in Baltimore. There they were all issued wooden mallets and shown to a large table covered with newspaper, where, as soon as they were seated, many large, steamed crabs were unceremoniously dumped in front of them. The sound the mallets made when cracking the crabs open was very like the sound Jonelle heard now, except that this was considerably louder, and the crabs in Baltimore hadn't screamed. Stones fell down from the cliff, and the Chryssalid shrieked and fell away from her. As it fell, laser fire lanced out from one of the teams preparing to board the Lightning. The pieces caught fire as they came down, and lay there in the snow, hissing, burning, until more blowing snow put the fire out.

Jonelle landed, breathing hard, more from the shock than anything else. Two of the squaddies hurried over to her with the sergeant. "Are you all right, Commander?"

"I'm OK," she said. "Let's get ourselves stowed. I'm going in to make that call."

Jonelle made her way back to the cockpit of the Lightning and looked out as her people got ready to be boarded. She hit the comms control for a connection to Irhil M'Goun. "Dispatch—"

"Yes ma'am, Commander."

She looked out the cockpit window at the early, early primrose-colored light of dawn, creeping into the eastern sky. "We've taken down that large Scout," she said, "about fifteen kilometers southwest of St. Moritz. We'll need a strip team. What's the condition down there?"

"*We're secure down here, Commander. No damage.*"

"Other intercepts?"

"*One successful, one failed.*"

"What failed?"

"*A Harvester came through on the same trajectory as your Scout, Commander. There was nothing to send after it but an Interceptor, and it lost that.*"

"Where did it go?"

"*Lost, Commander. We haven't a clue. Sorry.*"

"Wonderful," Jonelle said, more to herself than anyone else. "Wonderful. All right, Dispatch, we'll be back in Andermatt shortly. Tell Commander DeLonghi I'd appreciate a call."

And she hit the comms button to close down the line, and began, softly, and with some virtuosity, to swear.

Five

*I*t took Jonelle the better part of the day to get post-sortie matters sorted out at Andermatt. Though the facility had been ready enough to have flight crews move in, she hadn't seriously thought that sorties would have to start so quickly—at least, she'd hoped they wouldn't have to, but that hope was clearly gone. *The aliens know something's going on in this area*, she thought. *I've got to do everything I can to keep them from finding out what it is, especially until that mind shield gets in.*

Once back on site, Jonelle got on the comms network and on the phone, and began hounding people—mostly about the mind shield, but also about more transfer troops to replace the people most recently injured or killed, and about quickly disposing of the various marketable alien materials they had acquired this morning. Irhil, as well, had had a couple of successful interceptions—a medium Scout and an Abductor—which put the base over its break-even point for that month's finances and left it with a surprising amount of spare cash. Jonelle was glad about that, for she intended to take most of it for Andermatt. She was gladder still that there had been no deaths during those interceptions and only a few injuries, none of them very serious. *Either Joe's finally settling in,* she thought, *or else Ari read him the riot act forcefully enough that he took it to heart, and the results are showing already. A little early to know which, yet, but we'll see....*

She sat awhile with her calculator, totaling up the funds available to her and considering her options. It was now more likely that Andermatt would be attacked, since an attack had been launched from it. *Not a whole lot more likely—but the threat is significant.* She had already budgeted for the simplest level of defense, missile defenses, and those were in the process of going in. They would be ready next week, but they weren't as effective as Jonelle would like. Fortunately, the site itself was not terribly amenable to anyone landing there, alien or otherwise. Chastelhorn Mountain was one of the most nearly vertical-sided peaks Jonelle had seen hereabouts. However, that would not stop aliens attacking it while in flight. Plasma-weapon defenses would be better, but they cost a lot more, and Jonelle had just spent so much on the mind shield, which wasn't going to be ready for a month and a bit anyway.

She sighed. The missile defenses would have to do for the time being. There was also workshop space to be thinking about, and a new psi lab for Andermatt....

I hate this, Jonelle thought. *Here we are saving the goddamn Earth every other day, and nevertheless we have to drive ourselves crazy pinching pennies and skimping on equipment we need so that we can buy other equipment we need.... It's disgusting. We should have carte blanche, if we're supposed to function properly! I can just see it: about two centuries from now, some friendly alien species comes through here and finds our present bunch in residence, and when the new guys ask the invaders what happened to the original species, they'll say, "Oh, they died of insufficient cash flow."*

The commlink warbled at her. She slapped it, probably harder than necessary, and said, "Yeah, what?"

"Irhil comms, Commander," said her secretary Joel's voice. "Got your noon report."

Oh God, is it that time already? I've got to eat something before I fall over. "Talk to me," she said.

"Commander DeLonghi's compliments, but he can't make his own daily report until three. He's down putting the boot in on some craft repairs."

"That's all right. What else?"

"Got someone down in the infirmary asking for you."

"Joel!!"

"Says he wants to lodge a complaint, actually. Something about the quality of the food, or lack of it rather."

"How long has he been conscious?"

"About two hours, it seems. Doc didn't inform anybody until about half an hour ago. He wanted to run some diagnostics, he said, and didn't want the whole planet stampeding in there to see him."

"The doctor," Jonelle said, getting up hurriedly and

getting into her uniform jacket, "is going to get yelled at for not calling me first. You tell him so."

"*Yes, ma'am.*" Joel's voice was amused. "*I think he was expecting it.*"

"It's good to have staff who're prepared," Jonelle said, and slapped the comms control to shut it down. Then she headed down the hall to see how the second-level hangars were coming along—and to hitch a ride with the next Skyranger heading down to Irhil M'Goun.

She heard his voice long before she saw him. It sounded somewhat cracked and rusty, not much like the usual mellow rumble, and Jonelle paused just inside the infirmary's office door to listen for a second before making her way back to the bed wing.

"What total crap. You're just doing this to make me miserable."

"I'm doing this," said Gyorgi's patient voice, "because it is seriously unwise to overstress the digestive system of someone who's just had a skull trauma. I could explain the whole etiology of the problem to you, using short words and big color pictures, but I don't have time. Let's just say I have no desire to see you blow a blood vessel tonight, my evening off I might add, because I indulged your pathetic whining for chili. You can have chili in a couple of days. Right now, you drink the goddamn milkshake, or I'll dump it in your lap."

"I don't like strawberry!"

"That's not what you said in Rome," Jonelle said, putting her head in the bed-wing door.

Ari lay there in the bed, supported at a low angle by a couple of pillows, and turned on her the only slightly changed expression of generalized loathing with which he had been regarding the pink milkshake on the bedside table. He looked thoroughly disgusted and uncomfortable, and she was very hard put not to burst out laughing.

"In Rome," he said, "they were *fresh* strawberries, Commander. Unlike this wretched, artificial strawb-o-pap. Nothing that color can possibly be any good for you."

"The protein content is quite adequate," Gyorgi said, "for the temporary nourishment of the colonel's allegedly superb physique, and much more than adequate for the sustenance of the minuscule brain inside that foam-rubber skull. Drink it, Ari, because that's all you're getting until dinner." He headed out of the room.

"What's dinner? Beef-o-pap?" Ari more or less shouted after him, but the shout cracked and turned into a squeak halfway, as Gyorgi shut the door behind him.

"He's torturing me for fun, Jonelle," Ari muttered. "Just because I told him Crud was a dumb game."

"Serves you right." She pulled up a chair to the bed and glanced around her. "I see Molson's moved on."

Ari nodded. "He said to tell you he said thanks, and he'll be back."

"Damn straight he will. He's a good man." She looked at Ari and smiled, an expression that felt so odd, after the strains of the last few days, that she was amazed her face didn't crack. "And how about you? How're you feeling?"

"Like I've been tap-danced on by elephants. The usual, after you have a brush with *them*." Jonelle knew the feeling.

The use of the psi-amp itself was not without its strains and side effects, and when you had a mind-to-mind tussle with an alien, you tended to feel afterwards as though someone had been beating you with baseball bats—another result of the body's tendency to render psi-sourced traumas into physical terms that it could understand. When the alien got the better of the argument, though, the physical effects were much more marked—but Jonelle had never felt it fair to complain about this afterwards. She had been glad enough still to be alive.

"Has Gyorgi said anything about when you'll be able to go back on duty?"

"A few days, he thinks. But I am not going to survive three days of these." He gave the milkshake a look that should have shattered the glass.

"Yes, you will. You just do what he says—he knows what he's talking about. Remember Michaels, that squaddie who didn't come out of a coma for six weeks...."

Jonelle broke off, for Ari was gazing at her with a most peculiar expression. "What's the matter? Don't you feel well?" she asked sarcastically.

"I was going to ask you the same question. You look awful. You've got big circles under your eyes."

She laughed, just a breath's worth. "Well, I didn't get to bed until late."

"Overwork again. You're going to ruin yourself, Jonelle—"

"I was out drinking with the locals, actually."

Ari blinked. "You mean your yodeling partner?"

"Ueli Trager, yes, and his friends." Jonelle chuckled. "If the guys here ever get tired of Crud, I'm in a position to put them onto a new betting sport. Cow-fighting is more complex than you might think. I got about two hours' sleep before I had to go out on a run. Bagged us a large Scout."

"You had to go out on a—since when does the base commander do interceptions?"

"Since there was no one else available to handle it, and I had the necessary craft on hand but not enough other senior staff," Jonelle said. She then added, in a slightly more dangerous tone, "Which I might have had, had *you* been available. Of course, when a colonel disobeys a direct order *not* to go out and do interceptions, but to stay in one place where he can advise everybody...."

Ari suddenly became very interested in the ceiling, the milkshake, and the bed curtains, one after another. "Well. I wondered if that might come up. I—"

"Not today," Jonelle said, with a wry look. "Gyorgi would have my head, and rightly. But you and I are going to have a discussion about this at a later date. Yes, I've read the transcripts, and talked to the people you led out that night, and yes, I understand what you thought the case for going out was, and yes, you did a nice job in Zürich. But your job was not to *be* in Zürich."

Ari opened his mouth. Jonelle looked at him. Ari shut his mouth again.

"Quite," Jonelle said. "So let's let that rest for the moment. But yes, I'm pretty wiped out, and I won't mind the sight of my bed tonight...even though you're not in it."

Ari was still looking at her with a slightly astonished expression. "You were worried about me!" he said.

What seemed about a hundred possible responses to this statement went through Jonelle's head in the space of about three seconds. She threw them all out and simply paused to look at the statement itself, unadorned. Then she smiled again.

"Yes," she said. "But, for the moment anyway, I'm not anymore. You just lie here and drink the strawb-o-pap, and take the tests Gyorgi gives you, and do what's necessary, because I need you back in the saddle in a hurry."

He looked at Jonelle thoughtfully. "Yeah," he said. "OK. But Commander—"

She raised her eyebrows at him.

"I'm sorry about the Avenger."

"'Sorry' butters no bread, Colonel," Jonelle said calmly. "I'm going to have to take it out of your pay. Let's see: one Avenger at $900,000, plus fusion-ball launcher, that's $242,000, plus one fusion ball used, let's see, that's $28,000...."

"Wait a minute! The one I used worked! I fried a goddamn *Battleship* with it!"

"The use wasn't authorized. Well, maybe I can get you a discount. Let's say $20,000. The total is $1,162,000—"

"What about the materials costs on the Battleship! What about all those alien corpses, and all that Elerium—"

"Belongs to Regional Command, I'm afraid. Sorry, Colonel. So, let's see. Assuming you live another fifty years—"

"I'm beginning to hope I won't," Ari muttered.

"Well, think about it, it's not so bad: only $23,000 a year and some loose change to pay back. Plus interest on the debt—"

"Commander," Ari said rather desperately, "I feel fatigued. If the Commander would excuse me—"

Jonelle looked at him with what she hoped was an expression suggesting tolerance of a subordinate's unavoidable inability to cope. "Why, of course, Colonel. I'll drop by tomorrow, and we can continue working out the details."

She got up and made for the door, turning quickly to hide her smile. *He doesn't know how I'm going to handle this when he's better*, she thought, *and that's just as well, for the moment...because I don't know either.*

"But, Commander—thanks for the report."

She turned again, looking at him with slight surprise. "Which one?"

"The one you gave me the other night." He swallowed, and that big, prominent Adam's apple of his went up and down. "It was dark where I was...I was wandering around ...I didn't know where to go." The mere admission made Jonelle's heart wrench a little—he was always so certain whenever he opened his mouth. "I wandered around for a long time. I was so tired...I wanted to just lie down and not think about anything anymore. I almost did that. But after a while I heard something, someone giving a briefing, I thought, and I went over in that direction and stood outside the room. I thought it was a room, anyway. The voice was muffled, like someone on the other side of a door. It was you, giving someone a briefing. Then after a while I knew it was you giving *me* a briefing. So I stayed."

She swallowed too, and nodded, and turned again.

"It was a good briefing," Ari said, very quietly.

"Thank you," Jonelle said, as quietly, and left in a hurry.

Commander DeLonghi was somewhat surprised by the mellow mood in which he found Jonelle when they met. She was at some pains to let him know this wasn't simply because she had had an opportunity to go out and handle an interception herself, thereby blowing off some steam. She was genuinely pleased by the way he had set his teams up, making sure that everyone had the right weapons and equipment to deal with the specific threats at hand. She spent their hour together not yelling at him (as Jonelle knew very well he had expected), but going over his ship and troop assignments in detail to make sure that he did as well next time, or better. *I'm going to be up to my nose in Andermatt for the next little while,* she thought, *and the more positive reinforcement Joe gets from planning wisely and doing well, and being praised for it, the better.*

After seeing him, Jonelle went off to do her rounds— the first really leisurely tour of the base she'd had since the Andermatt business broke over her so suddenly. She found the usual Crud tournament in progress, and the pilots and assault crews shouted cheerfully at her as she came through, a sound that reassured her. These were people who were clearly settling successfully into a changed routine, feeling confident about it and about their results the night before. Jonelle had found a long time ago that success spawns more success, and failure breeds failure—the latter more quickly than the former, unless a smart commander moved speedily to nip it in the bud. DeLonghi would be discovering this himself shortly, she was sure, as soon as his own confidence was in place.

In the engineering areas and the workshops she found business progressing pretty much as usual, but spent as much time there as she had with the pilots and assault crews. It was imperative for the "support" end of an X-COM base to understand that it was as just important as the flashier departments, and that firing guns was difficult for anyone until they had first been built. The workshop staff, as usual, chaffed Jonelle for wasting any time at all with the pilots, when the really important side of business was taking place down here, on the assembly line. She laughed, agreed with them completely, and went on her way.

Jonelle left the alien containment facilities for last, as usual. It was simply not her favorite part of the base even under the best of circumstances. She swung through fairly quickly, pausing longest with one of the teams that was doing an interrogation on the Snakeman leader her interception had caught. In one outer office, two scientists and one of Jonelle's captains, Arwe Ngadge, were busy working on the alein with a mind-probe. The scientists were watching the readings from the probe on their monitoring console while Ngadge sat wearing a headset-mike and making copious notes on a legal pad. Behind the armor glass in the confinement module, the alien sat stiff, blank-eyed, and robotic-looking on the cell's little bench.

As Jonelle looked in, Ngadge glanced up and smiled slightly. "Commander—half a second." He took off his headset, handed it to one of the scientists, and said, "Look, try twelve and fifteen again—the responses to those were awfully equivocal."

The scientist nodded, and Ngadge unfolded his dark, seven-foot-tall self, got up, and went out into the hall. Jonelle peered through the windows at their captive. "Anything useful, Arwe?" she said.

"Hard to say until we're finished. But I confess that the thing I'm most interested in is why they had so many Silacoids aboard that ship."

Jonelle nodded. Of all the alien species that X-COM had had to contend with since the invasion began, Silacoids were probably considered the least threatening of the lot. They were not aggressive on their own—other species, usually Mutons, controlled them via telepathy and cybernetic implants. They looked like nothing so much as lumpy boulders, and their whole purpose in life seemed to be eating rock and dirt. True, they were annoying enough when they attacked you—which they did in a very straightforward manner: by throwing themselves at you, with about the same results as if someone had chucked a hundred-pound rock in your direction. But they were easily blown up, or shot up, assuming you had some form of ammunition that could pierce the coat of stone that was a Silacoid's skin. For her own part, Jonelle (when she thought about them at all) felt vaguely sorry for them, the only alien species that could possibly have provoked such a response. Their silicon-based physiology and their tiny brains suggested that the other, more intelligent alien invaders had simply picked the poor things up from their native planet, wherever it might be, and started using them as mobile, dim-witted weapons.

"When you send the stripping team up, Commander," Ngadge said, "would you have them do some scanning? I'd like to make sure that no Silacoids were missed in the shuffle."

"The way they generate heat," Jonelle said, "I'd have thought we would have picked them all up without any trouble. But, yes, I'll have it checked. Anything else from this gent?"

"Nothing much so far. Indications are that he was on a mission to an alien base somewhere—the hyperwave decoder records confirm that much. But where, or what it was about—" Ngadge shrugged. "At any rate, we'll keep working. This guy is a lot more resistant than some we've worked with lately, and I'm curious to see just why."

"Send a report along to Andermatt as soon as you have any ideas. Have you seen Jim Trenchard?"

"He's down in his office."

"Right. Thanks, Arwe."

Jonelle strolled down the corridor to Trenchard's office. He was sitting with the door open, as usual—she had often wondered how he could possibly work that way—humming to himself and hammering away at his computer keyboard. At the sound of her footsteps, he glanced up and said, "Commander! Got a moment?"

"Several." She came in and sat down, glancing around in slight amusement, as she always did, at the increasing number of articles, photos, and clippings pinned to all four of Trenchard's office walls. This was his filing system, apparently highly developed and effective, though it looked utterly chaotic. Pictures of elephants and pandas, and crayon drawings by one of his nursery-school-age nieces, were pinned over scribbled-on pages from *Scientific American* and *The New England Journal of Medicine*. Graphs and printouts mixed with handwritten notes and the occasional incomplete crossword puzzle. The only things on his two desks were books, piled up neatly, and a coffee mug full of pens and pencils.

Trenchard saved whatever he was working on at the computer, then leaned over to one side and started ruffling through some papers pinned to the wall. "I've got the initial research proposals and master schedule for the new place," he said, giving up on that particular spot and leaning over the other way to try another set of papers, half underneath a map of the solar system, on which some wag had written, pointing out of the system and (theoretically) in the direction of the alien homeworlds, "WRONG SIDE OF THE TRACKS.""Right, here we are."

He detached the sheaf of papers and handed them to Jonelle. She ruffled through them, impressed. "This whole thing? This must be a year's worth."

"Two."

Jonelle glanced over the chapter headings and subheadings. *Reapers: Floater liaison methods—defeating neural and cardiac redundancy—neural neutralization—aerosols? Sectoids: Neurocortical analysis—recombinant cloning: cloning "back to type."* Snakemen: *Remote sterilization techniques? Second-generation in ovo sterilization.*

"Haven't missed much here, have you?" Jonelle said, admiringly. "Ambitious, to say the least. What am I supposed to mortgage to afford all these scientists and researchers, Jim?"

"Well, nothing much, Commander," Trenchard said. "If you look at the costing analyses on the back few pages—that's right." Jonelle turned to them and found herself looking at a very professional estimate of the next two years' earnings at Andermatt, based on her first thirteen months at Irhil M'Goun, and showing estimated growth of the new base's income and ways in which part of that income could be used to fund the new researches.

"If I didn't know better," Jonelle said, "I'd think you'd been bribing my secretary for these figures."

"Hardly any need for that, Commander," Trenchard said, sitting back in his typing chair and stretching a little. "It's common knowledge in the base what comes in over a given week, in terms of Elerium and alien alloys and so forth. Notice that nothing much is said about outgoings." He smiled slightly. "Not my table, so to speak. But the market values of these things are all well enough known."

She nodded, put the sheaf of papers down. "I'll look these over in more detail...but if you're as effective at Andermatt as you have been down here, I'm hardly going to quibble. Who are you recommending I leave handling the supervision of research down here?"

He looked a little shocked. "I'd hoped to manage both

ends myself, Commander. There are things going on down here I'd hate to have to drop in the middle. My research assistants are OK, I suppose, but...."

"All right, all right!" she said, and chuckled a little, for he was starting to talk faster and faster, always a bad sign. "Look, Jim. Are you sure you can handle a load like that? I'd hate to have the researches down here wind up getting slighted while you're getting the Andermatt end of things up to speed."

He let out a long breath, then grinned a little. "It's always hard to let go, isn't it?" Trenchard said. "I'll reassess, if you like. But truly, Commander, I think I can manage. I'll have to delegate a little more at this end, is all."

"Good man," Jonelle said and glanced around the walls again. "So let me take this 'home' and look at it. Meanwhile, how's your own work going? The business I interrupted you in the other night."

"Pretty well. A lot more raw material to work with, lately, thanks to the colonel."

"Enough for your uses?"

Trenchard laughed a little ruefully. "I'm not sure a whole planetful would be enough.... Well, *maybe* it would...but it would still leave me with unanswered questions, I'm sure. The line of investigation I've been pursuing, the question of energy transport to and from the cells of the Ethereals' bodies, and specifically into and out of their brains, is probably going to elude us for a good while yet. The trouble is that you need to have clearly formulated questions to 'ask' the research material, and finding the right questions to ask...." He sighed. "The ones I'm stuck with right now are fairly general."

"Such as?"

"Well, the biologist's basic one, when looking at any new species. What do you have to do to a species, in the evolutionary sense, to make it turn out this way? That's the one that usually gives you a sense of where to start work, depending on your intentions toward the species in general—whether you want to help it be more efficient, or stop it, kill it. What trials, what twists and turns in its home environment, what disasters or encroachments from other species, can cause the changes from whatever the original form was to what you see before you? And how do those changes reflect on its life cycle now?"

Trenchard reached into a drawer and came up with a Toblerone bar, offering it to Jonelle. She shook her head. Trenchard nodded, then broke off a chunk himself. "There's a theory that's made the rounds," he said, more or less around the chocolate, "that the Ethereals might be a more evolved form of the Sectoid."

Jonelle had heard the theory but had no idea how much truth there might be behind it. "Have you found any proof that that might actually be the case?"

"Well, not *proof* as such. But there are similarities. Certainly the Sectoid evolution seems to be selecting some of its organic systems out, dumping them by the wayside. Already they hardly have a digestive tract to speak of. Certainly their kidnapping of humans for genetic-engineering experimentation suggests that they're starting to take a hand in their own evolution, these days, looking for human genes that will recombine successfully with their own, and one of their main interests has seemed to be in vascular genetics. Maybe the circulatory system is the next one they're thinking about getting rid of. Or maybe it's something else entirely."

Trenchard broke off another piece of Toblerone and looked thoughtful. "Whatever else can be said about this kind of minimalist approach to physiology, though, it may have its points. Look at the Ethereals. We're still struggling to understand what makes them go. I probably know more about the subject than all but three or four other people on the planet, and I'm seriously confused —expect to be for years. But Ethereals survive. There's almost nothing to them, yet they are incredibly resistant to our weapons. There's no way to tell how long their life-spans might be—except that I doubt they're very short— and the sheer power of their minds is incredible. Maybe less is more. Maybe this is something we should be looking at for humans."

He went on munching. "I mean, we come back, eventually, to the question: what do you do to a species so that it turns out like this? Interrogation of Ethereals is an iffy business, you know that, but when we press them about where they come from, we keep getting this image or tangential description of somewhere dim and red, very cold, empty.... Suppose their homeworld is circling a very old star? One that's way down the stellar classes, an N or R, mostly cooling gases. It would take a long time for a change like that to set in, and if the dominant species on the planet were sufficiently advanced, it could start making changes in itself so as to be able to survive...dumping the systems it doesn't need. As the homeworld starts to die along with the primary, suppose the intelligent species starts killing off the parts of itself it can no longer support? No more food? Easy: find some other means of energy transport to the body's cells, and kill off the digestive system once you don't need it any more. No more heat? Again, find another energy source and method of transport for it—maybe something like electromagnetic or gravitational fields. The same for light—engineer a new kind of sensorium, get rid of the old one. Even air, eventually—the earlier changes I've described would make respiration redundant, anyway."

"A creature so changed," Jonelle said, "wouldn't bear much likeness at all to its parent species."

"No. But it would have survived...and in this universe, anyway, survival is what counts. What hasn't survived doesn't count any more." Trenchard looked at the Toblerone bar, and his hands. "Now look at that—it's all over me. How can such tidy people produce such messy food?" He dropped the bar back in its drawer, then came up with a tissue.

"The thing is," said Trenchard, "our own Sun will do that eventually, if it doesn't just go nova—which isn't very likely. Stars in its part of the main sequence rarely go to the trouble. A long, slow cooldown is more likely, after some initial flares. If humanity is to survive such a fate—

which we might not—then we're going to have to change the physiology itself to survive. We might end up doing something very like what the Ethereals have done."

"If we did," Jonelle said, "would we still be human?"

"Depends on your definition of humanity," Trenchard said, chucking the tissue in the wastepaper basket. "But at least we'd be alive. We would have bought ourselves time to find a way to be human somewhere else—or right where we were. Even now, being human isn't what it was ten thousand years ago, or twenty, or fifty. We have been doing genetic engineering on ourselves, directly or indirectly, by populations pushing one another around, intermarrying, wiping one another out, over thousands of years. And we've been doing it to all the other species we've been able to get our hands on, for thousands of years already. Bacteria, for example: some domesticated to our use—like the ones that make cheese and wine—others destroyed, like smallpox, or bred to be more infectious, like biological warfare agents. Sometimes we've done it accidentally—look at the way the AIDS virus and the tubercle bacillus have potentiated one another, creating more dangerous kinds of TB. Think of domestic cattle, pigs, sheep, you name it, all bred by us from the original limited wild species, the desired traits kept, the undesirable ones culled. That's genetic engineering—just the kind you don't need microsurgery for. Six hundred species of dog, all bred by us from one common ancestor, but are any of them less dogs for all that?"

Jonelle shook her head. "I wouldn't know," she said slowly. "I'm a cat person myself."

"But sooner or later," Trenchard said, "if we last long enough, that's a question we're going to have to answer. How human are we going to insist on being? So human that we can't survive what time has made of our world? Or will we relax ourselves to the inevitable?"

Jonelle smiled and got up, stretching. One of the transports would be heading down to Andermatt shortly, and if she got started now, she could be on it. "Inevitability," she said, slightly amused, "is in the mind of the beholder."

As she waved at Trenchard and stepped out, he grinned back, and said, "Tell that to entropy."

Six

Back in the mountain above Andermatt the next morning, Jonelle allowed herself the luxury of sleeping late, just for once, and didn't get up until about nine. There had been no UFO sightings or interceptions the night before. *Thank Heaven for small blessings*, she thought as she stretched and yawned and set about getting herself ready to face the day.

She spent it, until about noontime, looking over the number-two hangar space, making phone calls and comms calls, and generally catching up on the paperwork end of business. When her desk was cleared—or rather, when everything she had started piling on her office floor had been dealt with, as far as possible—Jonelle changed into civvies and took the little "covert train" down into town.

The day was bright and sunny, and the whole town was full of skiers, chattering at one another in three or four different languages and generally making Jonelle's eyes hurt at the violent way their ski clothes' colors clashed. *I can't wait for a couple of years from now*, she thought, *when the styles will change and soft colors, or earth tones, or anything else, will be in fashion.*

The PR office was having a quiet day, at least relatively so. "The skiers keep mistaking us for the tourist information center," Callie complained to Jonelle when she came in. "I've had three different groups of people come in here and try to get me to make hotel reservations for them. I'm beginning to think we should go down there and get a bunch of brochures."

Jonelle smiled a little. "Maybe you should. I don't know if they'd like us horning in on their business, though."

"As long as we don't try to sell lift passes," Callie said, "I suspect we'd be OK."

Jonelle laughed and sat down to go through some of the paperwork that was piling up down here: mostly written complaints and protests at the "UN's" presence, left by local people. X-COM required that its cover offices, when such were opened, function like the real thing, so Jonelle or someone she delegated had to write letters to the people who had complained, explaining— exactly as if she *were* a UN representative—what could or, most often, what couldn't be done regarding the problems they were complaining about. She spent an hour or two dictating some of these letters to Callie and (when Callie's lunch hour came around) tapping them out herself. It was not work that came particularly easily to Jonelle, especially the part where she had to tell people again and again that there was nothing she could do to help them. More than once, she wished she could simply take a laser cannon to the whole miserable pile.

Nonetheless, Jonelle finished the work and felt insufferably virtuous at the end of it. When Callie came back from her lunch break, Jonelle happily left the office to her and went out to get a sandwich of her own from the delicatessen just past the hotel.

She never made it quite that far. Having paused to look briefly in the window of the bookstore next to the hotel, she turned to cross the street to the deli and saw Ueli Trager coming along the street. His expression was furious, and at the same time somehow tragic.

"Herr *Präsident*—" she said.

He paused and looked at her. "Fräulein Barrett," said Ueli, "how are you doing this morning?"

Jonelle thought that the exercise of "bedside manner" would help Ueli no more than it would have helped Molson the other day. "I'm doing well enough," she said, "but Ueli, you look like you just lost your best friend! What's the matter?"

The expression he gave her was grim enough, though there was a kind of surprise in it as well, like the look he had given her when she'd admitted to forgetting his cow's name. "I'm very upset," Ueli said, "and I'm going to have a drink. Perhaps you would like to drink with me?"

The naked appeal in that face, always so reserved and controlled, except for the other night, shocked her somewhat. "Not alcohol, this early in the day," Jonelle said, "but yes, certainly. Let me just have a word with my assistant."

She went hurriedly back to the office, told Callie where she was going to be if she was needed, and then made her way back to Ueli. Together they walked to the Krone, and Ueli led the way into the bar. They sat down at one of the old, scarred wooden tables farthest back, underneath an ancient, rusty plow that some decor expert had thought would look picturesque hanging from the rafters. When Stefan the barman came back to them, Ueli said, "*Kornschnaps, bitte*—a double."

"Just a cola for me." Stefan went off to fetch the drinks, and Jonelle said, "Without any beer, Ueli?" Most of the people here, she had seen, preferred to drink the local firewater as a chaser.

"I would like to get drunk," Ueli said with a bitter air, suggesting that he thought he might not be able to.

"Tell me what's wrong!"

The schnapps and the cola came. Ueli picked up the slim, straight glass with the schnapps in it, stared at it, and knocked it straight back in one neat drink. He put the glass down and said to Jonelle, "My *pugniera* is gone."

"Gone? You mean your cow? Rosselana? Where?"

"I don't know. Someone has taken her."

Jonelle took a long drink of her cola, hoping nothing of what she was thinking showed in her face. "Who would take your cow?"

"The same person, perhaps," Ueli said heavily, "who left four of my other cows—" He shook his head. "Stefan? Another, please."

"Left them where?"

"Not where—how. Left them in pieces, on the ground. Cut up. The hearts torn out of them."

Stefan arrived with another glass. Ueli took it, glancing at him. "Keep them coming. Fräulein, you may not understand how it is—"

"Jonelle."

"Jonelle. I thank you. We are simple people in our way, and probably city people would not understand very well how we feel about these things. Certainly our cows are our livelihood. It's either do dairy work, in this part of the world, or cater to the skiers. There's nothing else, really, not enough land to farm, we're too far off the beaten track for industry. But there's little enough grazing so that we can only keep small numbers of cattle, and when you keep them in small groups, when one man has maybe ten or fifteen cows, they become not pets, but work associates. You get familiar with them, you come to know their ways and their habits. You are friends. With a *pugniera,* who's smarter than the others, stronger, a creature that stands out a little from its crowd—even if the crowd is only cows—you become friendly indeed. It's almost like a shepherd and a sheepdog: each of you is doing the same job, though in different ways, on different levels. You appreciate each other. Now a third of my own small herd are gone. It will have an impact on my income, yes, replacing them will require a big capital outlay, yes—but speaking of 'replacing' them is idle: they were associates of mine. And Rosselana, not butchered like the others, just gone—" He stared at the table. "Human beings did not do these things. No human was near the lower pastures. It's those others, isn't it? The aliens."

Jonelle kept her feelings out of her face. "I've heard they do that kind of thing, yes...."

"So." Ueli looked grim. "Why they come here to us, now, I don't know. It wasn't like this last year. We thought all that trouble that people were having, terror attacks, we thought all that kind of thing was for the cities, that it would pass us by. History has generally done that," he said, and glanced up with a wry look as the third schnapps appeared. "That's why so many people here still speak Romansh, the old language. Conquerors might come and go, but these high valleys were too much trouble to send troops to. Tax collectors, yes." The wry look went ironic. "One prince might lay claim to your valley one year, another one the next, a bishop the year after. You would pay the taxes and not care too much who you paid them to. Eventually the conquerors went off and left us to ourselves, and we gladly stayed up here out of the way, and let the world pass us by. But this," he said, downing the third glass, "will not pass us by, I think."

Jonelle shook her head slowly. "As I see it," she said "you're right. They mean to take the whole planet, if they can. And isolated valleys are not isolated, when you can look right down into them from space."

"Well," Ueli said. "You are a UN neutral observer facility, you say. Can you do nothing about this?"

Jonelle opened her mouth to say *Sorry, I can't help*, and then she shut it again. All morning, she had been saying that about things regarding which it was, alas, true. But this was a different case.

"We have," she said carefully, "some people who are supposed to be expert in these matters. I can send for one or two of them, if you request it. What exactly would you be asking that they do?"

"It's not just for me," Ueli said. "But I would certainly like to spare anyone else the kind of loss I've just suffered. We don't like to complain, as a rule, but if there are more butcheries like this one, many people in these parts, those who don't work in the tourist sector, will suffer badly in the next year or two. If it could be stopped, that would be a good thing. Even if we could find out where the cows have gone that have been stolen, whether they are dead or alive...."

Probably dead, Jonelle thought, for she knew all too well what happened to cattle that the aliens kidnapped whole. *Poor Ueli!* But she nodded. "Certainly," she said, "the organization can send some people to investigate. They would need to talk to anyone who saw anything strange. We might need some language help, Ueli. The investigators wouldn't all be German-speaking."

"There are certainly people here who would help," Ueli said. "Jonelle, when could they come?"

"If I can get down to the office and make some phone calls," she said, "possibly even today."

Ueli nodded. "Let us start, then."

Jonelle left Ueli at the bar and went back to her office. There she spent about two hours on the phone and on comms. So un-covert an operation had to be cleared through her superiors, and it didn't go through easily, or without considerable opposition. There were some members of Senior Regional Command who felt that no civilians should have anything whatsoever to do with X-COM operation, that there were too many possible leaks from civilians to those who might be giving information to the aliens. Others, though, were more willing to listen to reason, and Jonelle knew where they were, and who. Once matters were settled with them, she went back to the bar and found Ueli there—surprisingly, not much the worse for wear, despite what she suspected were an appalling number of schnappses downed while she was gone. "We'll start in the morning," she said. "They'll send over three or four people from Geneva." "They" was she, of course, and the people would not be coming from Geneva, but from Irhil M'Goun "They'll need to talk to everyone who lost a cow or has had a mutilation or abduction recently."

"All right," Ueli said. "But what can they do?" Jonelle sat and looked at him over the glass of white wine that she had finally permitted herself. "In all honesty, I don't know. They can try to establish a pattern, they can try to keep it from happening again elsewhere, by notifying your government...." She trailed off. She suspected Ueli knew as well as she did that the government could do precious little about a threat that dove down on it from space.

"But it's got to be better than nothing," she said.

"You're right, of course," said Ueli. But he didn't sound terribly convinced...and Jonelle couldn't blame him.

*   *   *

So it was the next morning that four X-COM people, with proper "UN" credentials in place, turned up in Andermatt and began querying the locals. Jonelle told the investigators to leave no stone unturned, or at least to appear to leave no stone unturned. They went clear down the Urseren Valley, starting at the next town down, Hospental, and farther yet to Realp—to any of the major areas nearby where there was enough pastureland for people to bother keeping cows. One investigator stayed in Göschenen and worked her way up the Göschenertal, which was where many of the Andermatt cows spent the summer, there being a lot more green there than there was locally. Another went over the Oberalp Pass to little hamlets like Tschamut and Selva. To each of the investigators, Ueli sent along a local man or woman who could handle the Urnerdeutsch dialect that nearly everyone around there spoke, and who would serve as native guide and icebreaker. A lot of the people who lived in the area, especially those farthest upcountry, were intensely private, and not used to strangers. In fact, people from Andermatt tended to use a dialect word, *waelisch*, to describe people from Realp and Hospental. It meant "foreigner."

The team met in Jonelle's office in Andermatt that evening, with no obvious conclusions to show for its day's work, though there were indications that the kidnapping and mutilation problem was much worse than Jonelle had thought. One of her people, Matt Jameson, a statistician, had spread one of the Swiss topographic maps out on the wall and was sticking pins into it.

"The red pins," he said, "are mutilations. The yellow ones are cownappings. The orange ones are a combination of the two in the same incident. Here are the most local ones." Matt pointed. "We have mutilations up by Göschenen, at Abfutt, Schwandi, Hochegg, the Ganderenalp, and Gurst. These aren't sorted by time, by the way. I'll be adding that later—probably flags on these pins. Up here, north of Göschenen, we had a cownapping in Riedboden, another one in Band. Then farther up the valley, in Standental, one in Standen, one in Hochberg, one at Hoerli, another one farther up by the rail tunnel at Heggbricken, and the farthest one north, by Gurtnellen."

Matt paused, checking the map against the sheaf of papers he was holding and paging through. "On the west side, around the Oberalp Pass, we had a mutilation at Carnihutt, a mutilation at Pardatsch di Vaccas—" He smiled grimly. "Apparently the name means 'the place where the cows hang out' in Romansh. Another one at Missas Grond, and a fourth at Uaul." He turned a page of his notes over. "Apparently there are none too close to Disentis, the big town in the middle of the western side of the east-west valley—our mutilators seem pretty chary of being seen. All the mutilations have been in quite isolated areas, with peaks around them high enough to prevent anyone seeing them from any kind of distance."

Jonelle nodded, and Matt turned back to the map. "Now, the cownappings have by and large been in areas a little less remote. One near the village of Medel, here—

another at Caspausa, just on the other side of the Oberalp Pass. Another one just outside of Göschenen, which is surprising, and yet another at Vausa, which is nearly as large as Göschenen.

"No one involved in such an operation would want to be noticed if they could avoid it," Jonelle said. "Any increase in local awareness means the supply of cows will decrease."

"Now here," said Matt, "are the rest of the combination kidnappings and mutilations. Some cows were lifted; others were lifted, dissected, and dumped. Like Ueli's case, the other night, from the Urserenwald Alp. That one too was surprisingly close to a large conurbation. Then another one over by Vieler, between Gurtnellen and Göschenen. Over on the other side of the Furka Pass, one at Unterwasser, and another outside a town called Münster, at a place called Schlapf. And, interestingly, one down here in Valle Leventina, at a place called Quinto. A much better populated area—nearly two thousand people living around there. But again, the valley is narrow there, and the peaks so close together that there are at least a couple of places where someone could quite easily take cows and not be seen from the town, even though it's only half a mile away as the crow flies."

"All right," Jonelle said. "Matt, that's quite a lot, for one day's work."

"There are incidents we heard about secondhand but haven't yet had time to verify with the people who actually own the cows or the land involved," Matt said. "What you see here is only firsthand info. We'll doubtless pick up another ten or fifteen incidents tomorrow, if the stories we heard today are true. One blip, by the way: we have a place that was hit twice. Münster."

"Twice," Ueli said, shaking his head. "That *is* news. I hadn't heard about it."

"All right." Jonelle turned to Ueli. "But I just want to be clear about this. If Matt's data is correct, these mutilations and cownappings have been going on as close to you as Oberwald and Münster, just the other side of the Furka Pass, not ten miles away—and you didn't know anything about it?"

"Well," Ueli said, and shrugged and spread his hands. "That's the Goms Valley over there, that's another canton: it's Valais over there. We're in *Uri*. We don't exchange official information—that's private. And we don't socialize much with the Gomsers. They're a long way away...it's hard to get there in the winter, the pass is closed, you have to put your car on the train and take it through the tunnel.... Then in summer, we're busy. The tourists, and the cows.... And local news, you see, it mostly stays local...you don't want other people, strangers, prying into your business."

Jonelle raised her eyebrows, remembering the word *waelisch,* "foreigner," used, to her initial amusement, for someone twenty miles away. But in the old days, when the local mind-sets were first formed, twenty miles over the pass might as well have been two countries over. It was difficult to reach, the other side didn't really have anything you wanted, anyway—why go? Why talk to those people? Why think about them?

"I heard a story," Jonelle said. "Tell me if it's true—that some people in a village up in these mountains built a gallows to execute criminals on, and when a neighboring village asked to borrow it to hang a thief of theirs, the people in the other village said, 'No—these gallows are for *us* and our children.'"

Ueli nodded, wearing a slightly rueful look. Jonelle smiled at him and said gently, "You're really going to have to change your habits and start talking to each other, even if the people over the other side of the mountain are just from Valais, or Vaud."

She rubbed her head and looked at the map. "We'll have another run at this tomorrow. I've got some other things to take care of." Matt looked down, decorously, busying himself with his papers; the others looked in other directions, their expressions studiedly blank. "But Ueli, do me a favor. When my people go back to do more investigations tomorrow, I'm going to have them ask not just about cows that have gone missing, but strange occurrences. If people have seen odd lights, strange things they can't account for in the mountains around here, I'd like to know about it. I'd like you to talk to the locals here tonight too, if you would, and just take sort of a straw poll for me. Have people seen odd things, heard weird noises? I mean, if all these mutilations and cownappings have been the work of UFOs, of aliens, well, you know how people can be about such things. Often they don't want to talk about them. Well, maybe you don't know how they are about such things," Jonelle amended hastily, "and come to think of it, neither do I, but...see if you can draw people out a little bit. You'll probably have a little more luck than we *waelisch*." She put a slight twist on the word.

Ueli gave her a look that was ironic, but slightly impressed. "Well," he said. "I have to warn you, you may get more than you bargained for. This is not one of the most normal parts of the world."

Jonelle gave him back his ironic expression, with interest. "No," Ueli said, earnestly, "you really don't know what I mean. This part of the Alps, there are a lot of strange stories...people have been seeing odd lights and strange creatures in these mountains since they settled here, almost two millennia ago. You're going to have to be careful how you ask your questions. Otherwise, people are going to start thinking you want to hear folktales, local monster stories, about things like the dwarves or the *buttatsch*—"

"*Buttatsch?*"

"It's a cow belly with eyes," Ueli said, straight-faced. "A flayed cow skin, with the udders flapping. It glows in the dark. The thing comes rolling downhill at you when you're on some lonely mountain track, moaning and howling and speaking in tongues—"

"Check, please," said Matt, standing up hurriedly. "If we leave now, we can be at the train station before nightfall."

Jonelle laughed. "This is not something I want to meet. But—heavens, Ueli, it sounds like some kind of—alien—"

"Don't ask me," Ueli said. "I've never seen one, and I'm not sure I believe in it. But if you do see what looks like a glow-in-the-dark cowhide coming at you, I would take myself elsewhere. Consider it a public safety announcement from the local government."

"Believe me," Jonelle said, "if I see anything like that, I'll call for backup right away."

They broke up for that evening. As Jonelle strolled back to the train station with her people, one of them said, "Cow bellies!"

"I don't know," Jonelle said softly. They were on the sidewalk that ran through the middle of the park, and well away from listening ears. "Could it be that the aliens have been hanging around here for some time?...But let's find out some more about these strange creatures Ueli's been talking about—it might do us some good. Think about how long people reported skinny little, big-headed aliens being involved in their own abductions, and then we found out they had been dealing with Sectoids."

"All right, Boss...we'll look into it."

"The rest of you, keep on the mutilation and abduction end of things. I had no idea there were so many of them down here. I've never heard of such a concentration of events. I may have to go back down to Irhil tonight or tomorrow, but I want to keep this rolling. These people have been very helpful to us in a lot of ways...and I want to try to return the favor, just a little, even if it's only covertly."

She did indeed go back to Irhil M'Goun that evening. Repairs were coming along well on the various craft that needed them, and DeLonghi looked almost glad to see her. He at least had had a chance to get some rest and some planning done regarding his next strategies for what to do should the pace of interceptions speed up again. Jonelle, in turn, told him about the cow situation in Switzerland.

"We keep hearing that there's been a decrease in mutilations and abductions," she said, "but I'm not sure I believe it. I'm going to be a little busy at Andermatt tomorrow again, but if you would keep on it from this end, Joe——." She gave him a quick rundown on the bases whose data-processing people she had already talked to. "They think I'm nuts, Joe," Jonelle said, "so you might want to play it that way too—that you're 'humoring the commander.' But see what else you can find."

"I wonder," DeLonghi said, "if an increase in human abductions simply blinded the upper-ups to the cow situation? Or whether they've bought into a blip in the statistics, one that happened at the same time the human stats jumped? You could make a case that the Powers That Be would be pleased to think that cownappings and mutilations were dropping off while they had the human problem to consider...and you could also believe that their own statisticians might not be willing to rock the boat, if they knew which way the official wind was blowing."

Jonelle sighed and said, "Too likely to be true. Well, see what you can find out. Any paperwork for me down here?"

"It's all been shipped back up to Andermatt."

"Fine. How are you holding up, Joe?"

DeLonghi chuckled a little. "Better than I was. It can be a bit of a shock, I suppose, taking on command...."

"Tell me about it."

"You didn't show any signs of distress when *you* came to it, I have to tell you."

"That," Jonelle said softly, "is because I was doing absolutely everything I could not to let on. If I had given any sense of how frustrated and unnerved I was by the situation the way it was when I came, do you think that everybody in the place wouldn't have noticed immediately? Imagine the effect on morale."

DeLonghi nodded slowly. "You keep your chin up," Jonelle said. "Never show fear—they can smell it. And don't dwell on past performance. This has not been the easiest couple of weeks for anybody."

"Nor for you, I would think," said DeLonghi.

Jonelle shrugged. "I'm doing all right...I have a new toy to play with."

DeLonghi grinned. "So have I."

"Enjoy," Jonelle said, patted him on the arm, and headed out.

She went on down to the infirmary. Ari was sitting up in bed, looking better. He seemed to have stopped complaining about the food—but he had not stopped complaining.

"I want out!" he was shouting at Gyorgi. "I feel fine! I don't ache anymore!"

Gyorgi was standing across the room from him, scribbling in a chart. "You're going to lie there," he said, "until tomorrow, whether you like it or not. Isn't he, Commander?"

"Of course you're going to lie there, if that's what Gyorgi says."

"It's not fair. I'm perfectly fit and ready to fly!"

"The constitution of a great ape," Gyorgi said, sounding resigned, "and the brains of a gerbil."

"Far be it from me to disagree with a considered medical opinion," said Jonelle demurely. "How's the food today, Ari?"

"Better."

"I let him have the chili," Gyorgi said. "If he gets indigestion, serves him right. It won't hurt his brains now, such as they are."

"And how *are* his brains, such as they are? And the rest of him?"

"He can fly tomorrow," Gyorgi said. "I just want him to take another day to restore himself."

"I don't need any restoring. I'm in great shape. All I want is to get up. And I want some more chili."

"Shut up, Ari," said Gyorgi, hanging up the chart and picking up another one. "Commander, tomorrow morning, as I said, he can fly. And I'll be pleased to get him out of here—I need the bed. Complaints, complaints all day!"

"If the food weren't terrible—" Ari said.

Standing quite close by the bed, Jonelle bent down. "My lion," she said, "shut up." She raised her voice and added, "Anyway, it's just as well, for by tomorrow I'm really going to need you back in the saddle. Things to take care of...also, I want you to come along and have a look at the Avenger."

"They can't have finished repairing it already!"

"No, they can't. I want you to look at the pitiful thing and see the error of your ways." She scowled at him, but she couldn't hold the mood and smiled again after a few seconds. "I do have other flying for you to do. Your Firestorm is all right?"

"As far as I know."

"Good."

"What's DeLonghi going to say when you take another piece of equipment away from him?"

"Nothing much, probably. He's doing better." Jonelle grinned. "It takes a little while to get the hang of making bricks without straw, but he's shaking down nicely. As for you, if you're up in Andermatt about noontime, that'll suit me fine." She was determined not to push him too hard; even though Gyorgi said he would be back in shape to fly, there was a slightly harrowed look about Ari, one that suggested he had looked farther down into the abyss of that Ethereal's mind, and the abyss of death, than he would have liked to.

"I'll be there," Ari said. "Sooner, if the jailer will let me."

Jonelle patted his hand and left him, then went off to make her rounds. As she was moving through the base, the Klaxons went off, signaling an interception. Jonelle hurried down to the operations center and found everything under control: DeLonghi was already there, looking over the dispatch operator's shoulder. "Got a small Scout near Cape Town," he said. "Just the one...first peep we've had out of them for a while."

"Go get 'im," Jonelle said, "and good hunting!" She made her way back to the hangar for a ride to Andermatt.

As the Skyranger that brought her back settled into the hangar, Jonelle looked around and for the first time really felt herself able to think of the Hall of the Mountain King as Andermatt Base. It had the proper look and feel of an X-COM base now: busy maintenance people hurrying about, the buzz of voices, the underlying hum of big machinery. *Only a few things missing now*, she thought as she disembarked. *That mind shield.... Well, more than a few things, actually.* There was the small matter of better base defenses. But there was nothing she could do about those right now.

Jonelle sighed and made her way back to her office. Afternoon was coming on, and she had another meeting scheduled with Ueli and her "UN representatives." On the desk in her office, she found a sealed courier box with all the paperwork from Irhil M'Goun. She looked at it, briefly sorry (as she had been more than once, lately) that her secretary Joel still wasn't going to be coming up here for a few days. She had left him with DeLonghi to ease the transition, with instructions to train a replacement. *Oh well, it won't get any better by just leaving it here.*

Jonelle sat down and started to page through it. The fattest sheaf of papers in it was the transcript of the interrogation of the two Ethereals that had been captured in the attack on the Battleship in Zürich. She skimmed through it, knowing she couldn't take time to deal with it right now. It was the kind of thing that required slow, careful reading, especially since the transcript format always slowed her down.

The cover letter on it was from Ngadge. *Commander*, it said, *here is the first set of interrogation results on subjects B122 and B123 from the Zürich raid. Trenchard did this interrogation in company with Origen—he was one of the intelligence officers—and the results are particularly good. Trenchard seems to have a gift for this kind of work. Indica-*

tions are of some kind of major thrust going on in the southern hemisphere, among less developed and prepared countries. Also odd alien interest in Antarctica...? We are investigating this and will be following it up with subject B124, B125 in the next couple of days.

Something else that's working right, Jonelle thought with satisfaction. *The southern hemisphere, though,...* There had been talk among some of the statistics people that attacks in the southern hemisphere did seem to be increasing. Jonelle thought someone should look into it. Africa in particular was such a big continent that she wondered whether it was wise to have just the one base there. And it was possible that a South African-based X-COM facility might be useful. *Then again,* Jonelle thought, *God help me, what happens if I suggest it, and they tell me to go build it? Maybe I should just keep my big mouth shut.*

She changed into her civvies again and swung by the cafeteria long enough to grab a sandwich. As she ate it, Jonelle reflected that this was definitely becoming a proper X-COM base, for the sandwich was badly made and showed signs of going stale already, even though it had almost certainly been made only that morning. *Oh, well, maybe I can get something in town.* She left the second half of the sandwich there and headed off to the elevator, to catch what had now been christened "the Toonerville Trolley."

When she walked into her office in Andermatt, Jonelle found a level of tension there that she had never yet seen The office was occupied by all her assistants, their various local translators, Ueli, and about four other people, members of the cow-betting cartel that had been drinking in the bar the other night. Half of them were talking at the tops of their lungs, and the other half were listening with dreadful interest.

"*Gruezi mitenands*, hello, everybody!" Jonelle shouted, also at the top of her lungs, and some semblance of quiet fell, though she got a clear sense that it was temporary. "Would you mind telling me what's going on?"

Ueli came over to her. "Jonelle," he said. "You remember when you asked me to ask whether people had seen strange things? Well. Quite a few people have—strange lights at night, and strange noises. That's nothing unusual around here—we get those all the time." There was much nodding from the other men. "However," Ueli said, "just a while ago we had a phone call from someone who says he spoke to someone who said he spoke to a lady who lives up on the alp across the valley—Rotmusch, the spot is called, just under the Spitzigrat Ridge. She says—they said—well, the person who talked to the person who talked to her says—that she saw a spaceship, she *saw* a spaceship come down and take our cows from the alp the other night!"

"You mean she saw it take your cow? Rosselana?"

"Well, it sounds like it, yes. The problem—" He looked embarrassed. "Jonelle, you must forgive me, there is no politically correct way to say this. She's a crazy lady. She's been telling everybody about howling ghosts and monsters in the ravines for years. To hear her say that she's seeing spaceships now, well, maybe she's just changing a little with the times—"

"Ueli," Jonelle said, "eyewitnesses may sometimes see more than they suspect. Don't you think we should go talk to this lady and see what she has to say?"

"Well, it's up to you. It's not easy to get up there. The road doesn't go all the way, it stops and there's just a foot track for a mile or so. Anything heavy has to go by the wire-elevator, it's so steep." Jonelle had seen these contraptions before: wire pulleys with electric motors attached to them. The motors would pull themselves and a pallet of cargo along a wire strung between two points; this was a favorite way of getting things up to otherwise inaccessible chalets and huts in the mountains, and the presence of one suggested immediately how easy—or not—it was going to be to get to a certain place.

"I think we should go see her," Jonelle said. "Assuming that she'll see us. Is she going to take kindly to having strangers come out of nowhere to grill her? Does she have—" Jonelle stopped. Local etiquette suggested that it was impolite to inquire too closely about your neighbors' weaponry or how much of it they had; this was a private matter.

"Oh, she's safe enough. She might shoot you with a crossbow, but not with a gun."

"I feel much safer," said Jonelle. "What's the best way to go?"

"We can take my four-wheel drive up," Ueli said. "That last mile, though, we'll have to walk. Or climb, rather."

"As long as you don't make me go up on the cargo pulley. Who else—" She looked at her statistician. "You, I think, Matt. Geneva might want to hear your take on it. Let's go."

*   *   *

Ueli had not been exaggerating when he said the run up would be difficult. They left Andermatt on the back road that led out of town past the pilgrimage chapel of Maria-Hilf, and went under the train tracks and the main road just past the train station. The road went across a small bridge over the river Reuss, its banks there reinforced with concrete to prevent flooding from the glacier-melt in the spring, and then started to climb the far side of the Reuss's flood plain and up onto the lower walls of the Spitzigrat Ridge.

They passed a few houses and a farm, and then the road gave out and turned into a rocky track, a narrow switchback trail that zigged and zagged back and forth across the face of the ridge. Jonelle hung on tight as the ride got more and more jarring. Biggish stones were all over the track, and more of them fell down onto it as they passed, as she watched. Ueli drove like a man who knew the road well, but this was no particular consolation to Jonelle. There were no guard rails, and the hairpin turns at the end of each straight stretch of the road showed that it was an appallingly long way down, and getting longer all the time.

This road ran into another, after about twenty bone-shaking minutes—a road patched with snow and ice as the lower one hadn't been, and with snow piled on either side. "Odd to see this here," Ueli said conversationally as they turned north, onto the other road, and started to climb again, "but this spot tends to hold the snow. The ridge top is practically scoured clean, at the moment. It's the wind."

"Tell me about it," Jonelle said, shivering. Ueli smiled tolerantly and turned the heat up.

Very shortly thereafter, this road, if one could grace it with such a name, simply ran out in a large field full of boulders. Upslope—a slope that topped out at least two hundred feet higher than the spot where they stood, if Jonelle was any good at judging such things—she could see a tiny, brown wooden house with the typical broad, shallowly sloping Alpine roof. The place looked to have been there since the Flood.

"It's about three hundred years old, that house," Ueli said, "maybe older."

"And this lady lives all by herself up here?" Jonelle said, looking around in bemusement. "She must have a heck of a time getting down to do the shopping."

"Ah, she does well enough," Ueli said as they started climbing. "About twenty years now, since her husband died, she has been there by herself. People tried to get her to move down into town, but she wouldn't. She said she'd been moving all her life, and she wasn't going to do it anymore. She does all right, Duonna Mati does. She has money put aside so every few weeks she comes down to town for things: She hunts, too. She has wood for the stove, a generator for electricity if she wants it, a cellphone if she needs it. But she doesn't use the more modern things very much, as far as I know."

They kept climbing. Once or twice Ueli had to stop to let Jonelle and Matt get their wind. Finally, after about another twenty minutes, they came out on top of the ridge and found themselves at the edge of a small, incongruous patch of green, a grassy place that appeared to have been laboriously weeded of its stones and boulders over a long period. Off to one side, a tethered goat grazed the greenery, looking at them incuriously out of its strange eyes.

Ueli paused there and shouted, "Duonna Mati, *bien di!*"

There was no answer for a few seconds. Then the brown front door opened, and a woman came out. She was fairly thin, and very tall, with startlingly silver hair pulled back in a tight bun. She was wearing jeans and a plain red sweatshirt, and almost new running shoes. From inside came a faint glow, as if from a fire. She shouted back, "*Bien onn*, Ueli," and then added something else that Jonelle couldn't catch.

Ueli saw the look on Jonelle's face. "Romansh," he said. "She uses the old local language sometimes, but then so do a lot of us here in the southeast. She says we should come in and get warm."

"I'll drink to that," Jonelle said softly.

They went in. Shortly Jonelle found herself ensconced by an open fire with the others, in a one-room house that, though completely made of wood that looked much older than three hundred years, was nevertheless perfectly tidy. This was something Jonelle had noticed in every building she'd been in since she came to Switzerland: the astonishing cleanliness of them, apparently another of the national traits. As for drinking, shortly she found she had to do that too, for as soon as she and Matt and Ueli were seated by the fire, Duonna Mati presented them all with small, thick, green-clear glasses of some clear liquid. Jonelle sniffed it, and smelled plums, and alcohol.

"She makes it herself," Ueli said encouragingly.

Oh wonderful, Jonelle thought: *a moonshiner*. Nonetheless she lifted the glass, toasted her hostess, and said "Viva" as they had taught her the other night in the bar. Then she knocked the glass back in one swoop.

The old woman looked at Jonelle and nodded an approving expression. Seen more closely, it was plain she had been beautiful when she was younger. Now her face was a mask of fine lines, out of which brilliant, vivid green eyes looked, examining Jonelle minutely, then glancing at Matt. Her hands were very gnarled, so much so that Jonelle wondered if she was in pain. After a moment the woman spoke to Ueli, and he spluttered slightly in mid-drink.

"What does she say?" Jonelle said.

"She says," Ueli said, "that she knows you're from the people who're working with the government. She wants to know what you're going to do about her old age benefit, which they keep trying to cut."

Amused, Jonelle smiled the smile she had become good at this past week. "Please tell her," she said, "that I'll look into it, and if there's anything I can do, I'll try to help. But I'm not sure there's much I can do."

The old woman eyed Jonelle with an expression that suggested she recognized bureaucratic bull when she heard it, but she smiled slightly. Then she spoke again. Ueli listened attentively, then said, "Duonna Mati says, if you can't do anything about that, what do you think you're going to be able to do about the spaceship that's stealing people's cows? *My* cow, she says."

Jonelle opened her mouth, closed it again. "Well," she said, "please ask her if she could possibly describe this spaceship to me."

Ueli translated the request. The old lady spoke briefly, measuring out distances with her hands, and Ueli said, "She's describing something that would be—oh, I'd say the size of two tractor-trailer trucks laid end to end. Octagonal and three stories tall, she says. She saw it quite clearly, though by moonlight. She was up late."

The old lady held her hands up to Jonelle and made a motion as if trying to flex them. Jonelle nodded. "I see. What did the ship do?"

Ueli translated this. Duonna Mati spoke in a low voice, then glanced out the window for a moment, into the dusk. "She says it came low from over the mountains, from southward. It came down to the field and landed, and people—creatures, rather, creatures in shells of some kind, she says—came out of it and took the cows. Some were small, like *'nanin,* like dwarves or children. They came out, and some took the cows into the ship. Then after awhile"—and here Ueli's face worked, while Duonna Mati spoke again—"they threw pieces of these cows out of the ship, onto the ground. The ship rose up and took off again."

"Forgive me," Jonelle said, "but I have to ask. Your alp is nearly two miles away. How could she have seen anything so clearly, at night, at this distance?"

Ueli translated the question.

The old lady smiled, got up with a creak of joints, and went over to beside the head of the carved wood bed.

There was a tripod standing there, with something fixed to the top of it. She brought the tripod back, standing it beside Jonelle.

Jonelle looked at the top of the tripod. Fastened to it was a pair of battleship-bridge binoculars: army surplus, and over fifty years old, but well taken care of—25 x 100s, with built-in filters. "My lord," she said, "that answers *that* question. If there were cows on that alp, she could have read the names written on the cowbells with these." She nodded at Duonna Mati to go on. *Plainly she saw the Harvester that they lost the other night.* "Where did it go? Did she see?"

The old woman nodded, understanding, and spoke. Ueli said, "It rose and flew after a while. But it didn't go far. She says—" He paused, like a man who thinks he's about to translate something quite mad. "She says she saw it go into the mountain."

Jonelle opened her mouth and shut it again, confused. Could Duonna Mati have seen one of her ships going into Andermatt Base? But how could she possibly confuse that with the Harvester, which she had correctly described?

Duonna Mati spoke again and got up. "She says to come, and she'll show us where it went in," said Ueli.

Jonelle followed the others out into the deepening dusk. It had been clear that day, but now clouds were riding up out of the west, catching the last light of the sun, which was already below the horizon. The sunset was spectacular even in its fading stages, and on the mountains to the east, Jonelle could see an effect that she had heard described, but never seen—the reflected light from those sunset clouds on the snow-covered mountains, which seemed to burn a deep, incandescent rose against the purple-blue of the oncoming night.

Duonna Mati led them over to one side of her property, where there was a better view of the Urseren Valley. All of Andermatt lay below them, its lights sparkling through the windy air. The old lady paused a moment, as if making very sure of her directions, and she pointed. "*Cheuora*," she said. "*Cheuora muntogna.*"

"There—that mountain," Ueli said. Duonna Mati pointed a little south of due east, not at the Chastelhorn under which Andermatt Base lay, but at a mountain that reared up high above a number of others, chief of a group that rose to it in a long south-pointing ridge.

"Scopi," Duonna Mati said, and Ueli nodded. "She's right. The mountain is called Scopi. It's a ten-thousand-footer down south of the Urseren Valley proper, just above the Lucomagno Pass. There's a lake there, an artificial one produced by damming the valley—produces much of the hydroelectric power for the area."

Jonelle shook her head, astonished. She turned to the old woman and said, "Please ask her to forgive me, but I must be very sure about this. Are you telling me that you saw the ship go *in* that mountain? Not just behind it?"

Duonna Mati looked at Jonelle with a serious expression, spoke to her slowly in her old language, as if to a child. Ueli blinked and said to Jonelle, "She says, 'I know you think perhaps I am mad. But I saw the mountain open, and the ship go inside. I saw lights inside, and then the vanishing of the lights. It was bright moonlight between the clouds, and there was no mistaking it. Not with those.'" She gestured back at her house and, indirectly, at the battleship-bridge binoculars.

No, there wouldn't be, Jonelle thought, *not with those. They were made for this kind of work.*

"Thank you," Jonelle said after a moment. The old woman said, *"Te' bienvegni,"* and turned to head back to the house.

They went back with her, for courtesy's sake, to talk just a little more and thank Duonna Mati for her help before leaving. But Jonelle's mind was abuzz, and Matt was looking at her with an expression of barely concealed horror. She could understand why.

Right on our doorstep, Jonelle thought. *Right in our back yard. An alien base, twenty miles away...full of God only knows what.*

What the hell do I do now?

Seven

Jonelle made her way back to Andermatt Base in a state of mind varying between panic and fury, but the chilly ride through the rail tunnel, with Matt watching her in silent assessment, steadied her mind. When she got back, she had her courses of action fairly well lined up.

The first thing she did was to look around the hangar to see what was there. Two Lightnings—that was good. And one of their pilots was there, doing a walk-around of his craft, preparatory to going out on a routine patrol. *Better still*, Jonelle thought.

"Ross," she said, joining him at the back of the craft and looking it over with him. "Getting ready to head out?"

"That's right, Commander. About fifteen minutes. Just routine stuff."

"That's fine. Could I get you to do something for me?"

"Sure, Commander. What?"

"I want to do an infrared survey of the mountains in the neighborhood," she said. "The weather people have been complaining about not being able to predict the air currents around here, due to some of the mountains being hotter than others, they say. We need to start getting a handle on it. When you finish your patrol—when will that be?"

"About ten, Commander."

"Fine. Take an extra half hour or so, and just have a high-level look at the mountains within a twenty-mile radius. You see any hot spots, make a note of them. I'd like to see your results when you get in. I promised Meteorology that I'd have some preliminary data for them tonight. Can you do that for me?"

"No problem at all, Commander," Ross said. "Anything else you need?"

"Not a thing. I'm going down to the cafeteria to see if I can get something fit to eat."

Ross laughed hollowly. "Good luck, Commander."

She waved at him and left him to his walk-around. Jonelle did indeed go to the cafeteria and did eat the food there, though she hardly tasted it. She chatted amiably enough with the staff and assault crews she met there, but afterwards she could hardly remember anything she said. She was watching the clock. Ross had left for his patrol just shortly after they talked, at about eight-thirty. Jonelle dawdled over her coffee for as long as she thought looked natural, then headed out to do an informal evening rounds. She stopped in the main lounge of the living quarters, where an incipient game of Crud paused. She looked at it, tempted, and then waved at her people and moved on. All through the base she walked, the finished parts and the empty ones, peering at everything. Her people greeted her wherever they met her, and Jonelle returned the greetings and went on, leaving behind her an increasing number of X-COM staff who wondered whether perhaps "the colonel" had had some kind of relapse. One maintenance crewman who saw Jonelle come into the hangar for the third time in twenty minutes, around ten-thirty that evening, later said, "I saw her *bite her nails*. You ever see her do that before?"

The Lightning that had been out on patrol landed shortly thereafter, and almost before its pilot was down the ladder, the commander was back. The hangar staff saw her and Ross stand together for a moment, chatting. Then the commander grinned at him, thanked him for the extra work, and walked off whistling. That at least looked normal, and the hangar staff went back to what they had been doing, shrugging at one another. "She's been under a lot of stress lately," said one of them. "Cut her some slack."

"Completely routine, Commander," Ross had said to Jonelle. "Nothing much out there tonight—at least nothing we're interested in."

He handed her a cassette from the Lightning's mission recording console. "I taped that IR survey for you," he said, "just in case the weather boys need extra detail."

"That was a good thought. Anything in particular stand out?"

"I'm not sure, Commander," Ross said, scratching his head. "Weather's not my area of expertise. There's one mountain out there, though, looks like it's got a hot spring under it or something."

"Oh?"

"Yeah. Mountain called Scope. No, Scopi—I just thought it said Scope at first. Funny name. Anyway, it reads about seven Kelvin higher than everything around it. A little higher in places, up to say eight point five. The air currents around there *were* pretty fierce."

"Huh," Jonelle said. "The geologists are going to have fun with that. This area wasn't supposed to be volcanic anymore." She sighed, smiled. "Well, thanks, Ross. I appreciate the extra time you took."

And off Jonelle went to her office, her mind already much calmer than it had been. Waiting for the other shoe to drop, that was always the hardest part of an operation for her, but dropping the shoe herself—that would have its own peculiar pleasures.

She went into her office, closed the door, picked up the secure phone, and dialed a certain number.

"Hallo?"

"Hello, Konni. It's Commander Barrett."

"Commander! What a pleasure. What can I do for you?"

"Just help me with a general knowledge question."

"Anything."

"What do you know about a mountain called Scopi?"

"A good climbing mountain," Konni said, casually enough. *"I know a lot of people who go up there for holidays."*

"Do you indeed? Well, I think I know a few, as well. Konni, *what's underneath that mountain?*"

"Uh. Commander, you know that kind of information is on a need-to-know basis—"

"Well, Konni, you'd better believe that I *need to know*!" she hollered down the phone. "*Because there is something in that mountain*! And unless you convince me otherwise, I am going to first tear that mountain open, and then blow it to kingdom come! If it's something of yours, then I want to give you a chance to explain. If it's not, then I've got the unhappy duty to tell you that you have squatters on your property—and if they're who I think they are, this call is to give you ample warning of what I'm going to do about it, so that your government doesn't become upset when I change the terrain of a small area in their Alps! And I *am* going to change it. *So you start getting me some answers*!"

There was a lot more than that to the phone call. It was interrupted for a while, so that Konni could go off and make a call on another phone. Then it resumed again, in a much more communicative and conciliatory style on both sides. After it was finished, Jonelle sat back, put her feet up on her desk, and felt briefly much better, for whatever was going on in that mountain, it had nothing to do with the Swiss government. There had been a facility there once, a long time ago, but it had been quite small compared to, say, Andermatt, and it had been closed for almost thirty years.

Jonelle explained to Konni that it was not closed anymore. Konni, speaking to her on the government's behalf, said that he, and they, understood entirely, and that if Jonelle needed to have something happen to that mountain, they would not charge X-COM for damage to their real estate. But they did ask that they be consulted when final plans were in place, so that a suitable cover story could be arranged.

That was all she had wanted to hear from them.

She did not go to bed that night. She stayed up in her quarters, working, working at the little desk, tapping away at her computer, making the occasional scrambled phone call. She would let no one into her office but people from the cafeteria, who she called every now and then to have them bring her sandwiches and coffee. This she did several times. The cafeteria staff were bemused, for she *ate* the sandwiches. "She's enjoying herself," one of them said to the others, "whatever she's up to. Maybe it's that the colonel's coming back in the morning.... She's trying to get the paperwork done so they can have at least one hot night without business intruding." This explanation was widely accepted, with much good-natured snickering.

Jonelle did not come out until about nine that morning, when she went straight to the number-one hangar. There she found a newly arrived Firestorm waiting, with maintenance people working around it. She said to them, "Is he here?"

"Yes, ma'am," one of them said. "Went down to the living quarters to get his place set up."

Jonelle headed in that direction and, opening one of the "blind" solid-metal security doors that led to the living quarters, actually bashed right into Ari, chest to chest, so that they had to grab each other to stay upright. The two of them reacted to one another, then burst out laughing while the people down the corridor hooted and applauded appreciatively. Ari backed off and saluted, Jonelle returned the salute, and they walked down together into the living quarters.

"Well, Colonel," Jonelle said. "How are you feeling?"

"Very well, Commander," Ari said. "I have something for you."

"Not right now," Jonelle muttered, with a slight smile.

"Not *that* kind of something. If the Commander will indulge me—"

"That's what I do mostly, I believe," Jonelle said.

Ari sighed. "I have a note for you."

"I would have thought we were past the note-passing stage," Jonelle said cheerfully, as they came to the door of Ari's quarters.

"Not from me," Ari said with exaggerated patience. "One of the people in the labs, in Xeno, asked me to give it to you."

"Why so hush-hush?"

"How should I know? I don't read your mail." They stepped through the door of Ari's quarters, and with it half-closed behind him, Ari took an envelope out of his uniform jacket pocket and handed it to her.

Jonelle looked at it, seeing her name written there in Ngadge's bold print. She opened it, pulled out the several sheets, and stood there in the doorway with her back mostly to the hall, reading them.

When she looked up at Ari again, she was feeling physically weak. "What is it?" he said, seeing the unnerved expression on her face. "What's the matter? Are you all right?"

She took a long breath, looked up at Ari, and shook her head, doing her best to get her composure back in place. "I can't discuss it," she said, folding the letter and putting it in her own jacket pocket. "It's probably not incredibly important in the big picture...and believe me, Ari, we've got more important things to think about. I'm going to need to talk to everybody here, and everybody at Irhil M'goun, at nine tonight, and I've still got to get the final wrinkles worked out of my script. You can help me best by telling everyone who asks you what this is about that you don't know."

"I *don't* know. I just got here!"

"Good. But one thing you could do for me that I would really appreciate—"

"Sure," he said, "what?"

"Make an appointment with me," she said, "for a few hours in the next twenty-four when we can get really, really physical." She smiled at him, a sad smile. "Because it's going to be a good while before we get another chance."

He looked at her, sobered by the tone of her voice. "I'll check my appointments calendar," he said, "and get back to you."

"Good," she said. "You do that."

That evening, about nine, Jonelle called the base complement of Andermatt together in the hangars, there being no other place that could hold them all. She also had a camera stationed to transmit her image into a scrambled link that would be shown at Irhil M'goun, where DeLonghi had also assembled everyone in the main hangar to hear what Jonelle had to say. Only DeLonghi knew what the content of the announcement was going to be. She had had a long, quiet talk with him about it earlier in the day.

She stood up in front of the camera and tried to look easy, though she didn't feel so. Public speaking was not one of Jonelle's great gifts. "This is Commander Barrett," she said. "X-COM Main Command has asked me to make the following announcement to you, as many other X-COM base commanders will be doing to the bases under their control about now.

"X-COM has located what may be one of the oldest alien bases on Earth, hidden away in a location where its presence has been unsuspected for what may have been years—we don't know for sure. Preliminary reports— based on analyses of all spacecraft trajectories that have occurred over the last year and a half—have identified the base's location as somewhere in the Carnic Alps between Austria and Italy, in a spot that I'm not going to identify exactly to you at the moment because there's no need.

"X-COM has decided that as soon as Andermatt Base is fully operational—which will be about three weeks from now—we will be the staging area for an assault on the alien base. This is going to be an assault of considerable size and difficulty, since we suspect that base to be 'dug in' to a mountain, similar to the way Andermatt is.

"This assault will have to be swift and well-organized to be effective. Planning of the details has already begun and will be complete by the time Andermatt Base is ready to stage it. That said, I intend to bring both Andermatt and Irhil M'goun bases to their highest possible levels of readiness by the approximate assault date three weeks from now. This announcement is in the nature of an early warning, to help you start work on achieving that readiness. Unusually rigorous drills and exercises, to prepare us for this assault, will be starting next week. I will be publishing details within the next day or so.

"You are all going to be asked to work very hard. Not harder than you're able to—and I refuse to work you harder than I'll be working myself. But you know how I work." Jonelle grinned, and a good-natured groan went up from the listeners at both Andermatt and Irhil M'goun.

"We're doing a good thing here," Jonelle said. "Many of the alien attacks that have so bedeviled us for the past year are thought to have come from this hidden alien base. By destroying it, we'll be buying ourselves and other bases time to prepare ever more effective weapons and strategies against the invaders...and to follow them, eventually, to other hidden bases, and possibly even to their base out in the solar system, wherever it is. But that's for the future. For the meantime, you'll liaise with your captains and sergeants to find out what each of you needs to do during this preparation period. And I want you to know that I'm going to be leading this assault from the front. We will go in together; as many as possible of us will come out together—and the aliens will come out only as prisoners, or corpses. That's the goal."

Jonelle looked briefly uncomfortable. "We have a planet to protect. A lot of our friends have gone out to do that, come up against the aliens, and not come back. This will be our chance to even the score a little, on their behalf—for the failed interceptions counted as much toward finding this hidden base as the successful ones did. So—let's get on with it."

She turned and walked away from the camera, gesturing at the tech person to cut the link. Applause started behind her—softly, at first, then louder. Jonelle held her head high and kept walking. There was only one thought in her mind at the moment:

Please, God, don't let me have to spend all their lives on this. Please don't make me kill them all.

Much later that evening, after a session of being very, very physical, Jonelle sighed and lay back with an absent look. Ari padded over to the bed, on his way back from the bathroom.

"I see Ross has been transferred," he said. "I'll miss him—he was a good man."

"Family emergency," Jonelle said, gazing thoughtfully at the wall. "He'll be back next month."

"'Family emergency'?" Ari said. "He doesn't have any family. Hasn't for years now."

Jonelle looked at him in the dimness of the one little lamp, then blushed a little and looked at the floor. "Ah. Well."

"The trouble with you," Ari said, "is that you're not a good liar."

She glanced at him swiftly.

"About personal things, I mean," said Ari. "Professionally, you can lie with the best of them. Can't you?"

"For the next week and a half," Jonelle said softly, "that's a thought I would keep to myself. Are you asking me to take you into my confidence?"

Ari took a long breath. "No."

"Good," Jonelle said. "There are, however, some things I want to discuss with you." She got up, went over to where her uniform jacket hung over the chair, and fished out the letter that Ari had brought her. "Take a look," she said.

He opened it and began to read. Jonelle sat back down on the bed and pulled the covers up, huddling under them for a moment.

"...Have for some time suspected that some colleague's experiments were of a rather odd nature. In particular, some serology projects being stored in the communal cold storage area have peculiar labeling anomalies, apparently being attributed to people whose experiments they were not. Some of these containers contained human blood serum samples that, on closer examination, show profound shifts away from the usual acid-base codings present in human blood and serum DNA. Some tissue samples that I had a chance to examine briefly, but which have since disappeared, show similar changes." Ari turned the page. "About a week ago, the absence of one of the research staff from the base on other business permitted me to examine these samples in more detail. While hardly being expert in this particular area, I can safely say that these samples indicate research along the following lines: Investigation into the blood serology of Ethereals. Investigation into the neural tissue serology of Ethereals. Investigation into the storage locations of lower cerebration facilities and the 'memory trace' in Ethereals. I have not been able to find any notes or other written material to substantiate further my investigations, but my guess is that all these researches are pointed toward a single purpose, and this is evidenced by one tissue sample I examined that has since disappeared: the progressive genetic alteration of human neural and blood tissue into Ethereal neural and blood tissue, by chemical means, by forward recombining of DNA and use of so-called 'rogue' and 'interweave' strands of messenger RNA, to construct a 'bridge' sequence between human and Ethereal genomes. The end product seems to be tissue of originally human provenance, but altered by the assisted action of Ethereal DNA, and various 'semi-viral' mechanisms—making material that would be, in essence, more Ethereal than human, and which in contact with other human material would derange it similarly. Such experimentation, while not strictly unethical if the material was locally derived, still strikes me as both dangerous and inappropriate for our facility. I must therefore advise you that I believe Jim Trenchard must be considered a security risk until more or better information can be obtained on exactly what the thrust of his research is."

Ari put the letter down, looking distinctly pale. "Trenchard," he said. "What's he doing?"

Jonelle wrapped her arms around her knees and put her chin down on them. "I think he's working on turning humans into Ethereals," she said.

"He's stark, stinking, blinking *nuts*!"

"No, I don't think so. I think he's sane...and that's the problem." She sighed. "Ngadge sent me a report on interrogations Trenchard was helping with. Said they were going a lot more smoothly since he started working on them. He was getting better results, somehow...the aliens were spilling more material...." Jonelle shook her head. "Are they spilling it because they were *sent* to do that?"

Ari lay back against the pillow, looking confused. "You lost me."

"I'm not sure it makes a whole lot of sense myself. But haven't you noticed we've been catching a whole lot more Ethereals lately?"

"We catch what we can," Ari said. "It's chance...isn't it?"

"Who decides crew complements on alien ships?" said Jonelle. "We don't know. How do we know for sure that some of the interceptions we've been making haven't been *allowed* to happen?"

"Oh, now, wait a minute! Are you saying that my *Battleship* the other day—"

"Maybe not the Battleship, but certainly some of the others. Ari, we really have come up with an unusual number of Ethereals lately. Who's helping who, here? And that other line in Ngadge's letter: 'If the material was locally derived—'"

Ari looked at Jonelle. "You mean from someone here—"

"I mean from Trenchard! It's the old joke for a geneticist: the version of the human genome that you're most familiar with is your own! These days, in any good four-year course in genetic engineering, one of the first things you do, practically, is take a strand of your own DNA—you own it, after all, it's legally safe—take it apart, look at your own genes, and see what's in their pockets!"

"Ouch."

"It *is* an old one. If he's using his own genetic material to experiment with—well. Those tissue samples that Ngadge said were already showing significant drift toward the Ethereal. Who's to say just how human Trenchard *is* anymore?"

"And he's been doing all these interrogations," Ari said, musing. "Who's been interrogating who?"

Jonelle nodded. "My thought exactly. He *likes* them, Ari. It's something I don't think I really saw until the other night...and then I thought it was just a quirk. It bothered me so much, I couldn't see it right away even then. *He likes them.* He said to me, 'This is something we need to look at for human beings.' He really thinks that their way of existence is an option for us."

"Effing traitor," Ari muttered. "He needs to be shot."

"No," Jonelle said. "That's the one thing we can't do."

"Whaddaya mean 'can't'? One bullet would do it. I must have a gun here somewhere." He made as if to get out of bed.

She pulled him back down. "No, if he is a spy I want him right where he is. The thing to do with a spy or a traitor is to give him the mushroom treatment."

"Sorry?"

"Keep him in the dark and feed him shit. But most importantly, don't let him know you know he's a spy. Trenchard will feed our disinformation to his friends among the aliens, which suits me just fine. And I'd like to know how he does it. I'm having comms monitored...but it's occurred to me that there might be other ways. Neural tissue...." She leaned back against the pillow, against Ari. "Supposing that he's managed to acquire some of their telepathic ability? If information about this projected raid gets to them via that route, and there's no trace in comms, we'll know that's how he did it. They might be able to read him like a book if he comes out from under the mindshield. That would be worth knowing about... and if it works for him that way, maybe he'll have discovered a weapon we can use on our own side, later. There'd be a nice irony in that."

She smiled grimly. "But no matter how they get the information, the aliens will know there's no base where I've announced it. I'm sure they'll be delighted to let us go off on a wild goose chase and attack some mountain with nothing in it, instead of the one I've already had some preliminary scans done on, the one that's full of the Silacoids they've been importing, and which have been tunneling it out for God knows how long. What they *won't* know, until too late anyway, is that we know exactly where they are, and that we're going to hit them a week and a half *before* I said we were. Other X-COM commanders have, indeed, made the same announcement I made tonight. It's not just to back up my story: Main Command is interested in finding out whether other bases have spies working in them. We'll see where this disinformation surfaces, and in what shape. Meantime, your business, and the other colonels', and mine, is to make sure...in the most easygoing and casual kind of way, without it particularly showing...that the attack is ready to happen a week and a half before the announced date."

"And what about Trenchard?"

"The day the balloon is really scheduled to go up," Jonelle said, "I'll be having him arrested and held incommunicado until it's all over. Then I'm going to come down and debrief him myself. Possibly with a nail file."

Ari looked at the expression on Jonelle's face, and swallowed.

"I'm beginning to regret ever having brought him to Andermatt," she said. "He knows where it is, and I can only assume that *they* know where it is. Our survival so far rests on two factors: that Trenchard doesn't know the exact locations under the mountain of some of our facilities here, and maybe the aliens don't want to risk exposing their spy. By the time they realize we're on to him...it'll be too late for them, or at least for their base under Scopi."

Ari nodded. "Weird name," he said. "What does it mean?"

Jonelle smiled in grim amusement, as she had when asking Duonna Mati about this through Ueli, and closed her eyes. "It means 'target.'"

A week and a half passed, and there came the only day of the week when even the Swiss sleep late: Sunday morning. Having gone to town early on another Sunday to look into some other matter, Jonelle had found herself wondering how they managed it. The chapel at the bottom of town, Saint Peter's and Paul's, and the one at the top of the town, Saint Kolumban's, began ringing their bells at eight forty-five, in what Jonelle could only describe as "dueling churches," a four-toned fight that went on deafeningly for half an hour, and certainly left everyone in town wide awake. It was, Jonelle had been told, traditional: not only an announcement that church services were about to start, but a sure remedy against demons, which could not stand the sound of bells. Much earlier than bell-time on this particular Sunday, though, Jonelle had set about her business: exorcising the local demons, as permanently as possible.

It went off like clockwork, in the initial stages—almost precisely like clockwork, for Jonelle had started to work out the timings on that first night when she came back from Andermatt after seeing Duonna Mati, and since then she had had plenty of time to refine them.

Everything would have seemed quiet enough, in the dawn. In those mountain fastnesses, in fair weather, dawn can be unearthly still: not a whisper of wind to blow the snow out into the "banner" that so often streams from the sides of mountains like Scopi, not even enough to trigger the veil of mist caused by the differential in temperature between the air updrafting along the mountainsides and the colder air above. In the silent dawn, Scopi reared its graceful peak against a sky of the purest pellucid royal blue at the zenith, fading down to crimson-rimmed peach at the jagged horizon, and everything held its breath and was still.

The sound that slowly leached into the silence, breaking it, echoed from the walls of Piz Rondadura and Piz Gannaretsch and all the other mountains around: a high, singing whine, slowly growing stronger, scaling up like the screech of an increasingly angry eagle. Nothing moved on the mountain in any kind of reaction; nothing lived there to move. But the screech grew more deafening, echoing more loudly from the mountains around and, abruptly, a flash of motion appeared from the south to match it.

It was a single Avenger, coming low along the treacherously wiggly line of the Lukmanïer Pass, zigging and zagging madly from one cliff-bound wall of the pass to the other, as if the pilot had had too much to drink the previous night, or wanted to look as if he had. At the southern end of Lai da Sontga Maria, the Avenger dove straight toward the surface of the lake and skimmed along it so low that an unprepared observer might have thought the pilot was about to take up powerboating. The thin skin of ice on the water cracked under him from the noise of his engines and the pressure of their thrust. Twin plumes of water burst up and out of the lake behind the Avenger as it skimmed along the length of it, no more than three feet above the lake's surface, and seemingly made straight for the automated hydroelectric dam at the northern end. At the last possible moment, the Avenger's pilot pulled up in what could have passed as the second leg of a right angle, and headed straight for the zenith.

Now the mountain spoke. Plasma fire burst from the eastern and southern sides of it, lancing out at the Avenger—but the pilot had other ideas. The Avenger angled around hard toward the northeastern side of Scopi, the one most nearly vertical. His craft made a sound like a giant cough, and a fusion ball leaped out from it and struck the mountain right in the middle of the slope called Puoza. In a great bloom of lightning, fire, and snow vaporized instantly and explosively to steam, the side of the mountain blew in.

There had been a door there, once, clearly marked in infrared view by an eye-shaped hot spot. The main question about this door had been, was it hardened? When the smoke and steam and the fire of the fusion ball cleared away, the answer was plain enough. Metal still showed there—badly buckled, but still not breached.

A routine had been prepared for this possibility. About six different craft descended on the mountain from all directions, peppering it with missles, plasma beams, and cannon and laser fire. More defensive fire erupted from the mountain and the attacking craft veered and dodged, trying to keep from destroying one another, as well as from being destroyed themselves. At least with the mountain's exit door damaged, there seemed no danger of alien ships coming out, so for the time being, the attacking X-COM vessels busied themselves with targeting the aliens' defensive facilities. One Interceptor took a direct hit up its six, and it and its pilot went out together in a spectacular fireball that crashed on Scopi's slopes. The snow went black with ash, where it wasn't scoured off the mountainside by the heat. Twisted wreckage tumbled down Scopi's side and fell steaming into the lake.

But only a second or so later, the Avenger—with Ari in the driver's seat—came roaring 'round the mountain and let the "front door" have it with another fusion ball. A globe of lightning crashed into the mountainside, clinging there, random discharges forking and flickering from it— and this time, the door blew into fragments. When the steam and the fireball cleared away, all that remained of the door was a jagged, metal-edged hole. The Avenger dove away to the north, executing a virtuoso victory roll complete with showy but unnecessary hesitations every ninety degrees.

In the cockpit of the Lightning from which she was leading the attack, Jonelle grinned evilly inside her armor and said softly down her commlink, "Go."

Their full complement of craft went in: everything from Irhil M'goun, everything from Andermatt, everything that Omaha and China could spare them. This was just as well, for immediately thereafter, all hell broke loose as alien ships leapt out of the ruined, but somewhat widened, opening. Small and medium and large Scouts, an Abductor, a Terror Ship.

Between the Abductor and the Terror Ship, like a swallow diving between two eagles, the Avenger, twisting and sliding between bursts of fire from the mountain, angled in and went straight through the blasted door. People on one Lightning in the attack group, and on others if they chanced to be tuned in to the commander's chat frequency, were almost deafened by a furious shout of "*You utter asshole, what the eff are you* doing!"

While the aerial battle went on outside, several other ships followed the Avenger in—these by design, instead of by opportunity. They flew into a huge, empty cavern filled with smoke and flying debris, for the Avenger had immediately fired at, and disabled, the Harvester ship presently sitting on the floor of the cavern. Weapons fire was also everywhere, but the X-COM ships put down regardless, opened up, and let their assault teams out.

Jonelle was with one of them. "By the numbers," she said down her commlink to the assault teams listening to her. "Pathfinders, go do your thing, and Godspeed. Immediate assault, with me—"

By the time all the craft were empty, there were about thirty X-COM people, all in either power or flying suits, on the floor of the main cavern, and all armed with heavy plasmas, small launchers, or better—blaster launchers. They began by simply sweeping the place clean of every alien that got in the way. The problem was that it would not stay clean; more and more kept flooding up from the lower levels.

This was something Jonelle had expected. The scans she had managed to conduct, ever so quietly, over the last week and a half had shown her that Scopi was a warren of tunnels, chimneys, and deep-delved caverns. The upper level, the "hangar" level, would have to be secured first; then her people would have to work their way down. Securing the whole facility might take hours, and kill them all. They did not have hours to spend, or that many lives. It was Jonelle's uncomfortable job to decide when enough lives had been spent, and to call for the final intervention that would destroy the alien base and end the battle.

At the same time, they could not destroy the base before being sure that all possible information and useful materiel had been removed, that everything that could be saved *had* been saved. The scans had shown that on the first and second levels down, there were larger "delvings" that were probably labs and armories. These had to be sacked if possible, destroyed if not. Farthest down were tunnels, into which the aliens would probably retreat for a last-ditch defense. In those, Jonelle had less interest. They could, and would, be sealed by the last destruction. But that was a little farther along. By her timing, no more than an hour....

On the floor of the main level, everything was smoke, laser fire, plasma eruptions, explosions—the air and the stone shook with them. There was a huge crash off to one side as the Avenger came down too hard on the stone floor. It was perhaps just luck that it came down on a party of Zombies, all of which immediately died, hatching out many new premature but savage Chryssalids in their stead. A few of one of the assault teams got busy on them with incendiaries.

More aliens came pouring up, and Jonelle found herself, as always, with less and less time to think about her timings, and more and more aliens to shoot at. She had a small, intent bodyguard of five to protect her, besides her flying armor, and she had a heavy plasma. With that, she got busy. *I'm the cleaning woman*, she thought, and concentrated on cleaning the main floor of every alien she might see. There was little trouble about this until a big force of Snakemen came slithering and hissing across the floor toward her and her group, maybe fifteen or twenty of them at once. Jonelle lost track of how long these kept them busy. As fast as she and her team could burn them down, more Snakemen came, a little army of them, into the teeth of better weaponry than they carried, trying to overwhelm Jonelle and her team by sheer force of numbers. Numbers were not going to be enough, though. The bodies began to pile up around them, a wall of writhing, persistent snake meat with blasted-off patches of scorched and peeling scales flaking off them. That god-awful, sweet smell of burnt flesh somehow always reminded Jonelle of Chinese food, and always put her off it for days after a raid. After what seemed an eternity, but was probably only fifteen minutes or so, she and her team found themselves with a moment to breathe, and nothing to shoot at for a few seconds. "OK," she said, peering through the smoke and the tumble and scatter of destroyed craft and dead aliens, through which her people moved like deadly ghosts, firing at anything that moved and wasn't one of them. "Report. How are we—"

That was when something caught her mind by its scruff, and shook it. Irrational terror flooded Jonelle. The assault troops around her, her bodyguard, dropped their weapons and collapsed, wailing, shrieking with fear.

Jonelle froze with the immediacy of the fear. She had never been a screamer; she was the kind of person who froze when she felt death coming, and watched it, silent, her voice stuck in her throat. She watched it come now, dark, drifting along the floor toward her, over the rubble and the corpses: a shrouded form like an alien Grim Reaper. Something concealed within the dark robes veiling that form spoke, intimately, to her mind. Not with words, but the feeling said, *You know us too well. You know things about us that cannot go any further. Therefore, die.*

The hand of fear squeezed her heart. Jonelle gasped, trying to get her breath past the ice in her chest, the lump of fear that was growing, that would force the breath out of her body, the warmth out of her bones, the life out of her brain....

And abruptly the cold "hand" dropped her. While plasma fire racketed over her head, and stun bombs howled and smoke drifted by, Jonelle groveled on the floor, gasping, trying to remember why she was there and what her name was. She looked up—

—to see an armored form standing straight and still in the smoke and the laser fire, staring at the silent, hovering form of the Ethereal, which hung still and stared at him. Ari stood there, in his own armor, with his psi-amp. The Ethereal faced him. The air practically itched with the strain of the two minds grappling together—and then Ari laughed out loud.

"Sorry, pal," he said between gritted teeth. "The last one tried *that* trick. Now I know what to do about it!"

For a moment there was silence. Then the Ethereal wavered, turned to flee, and was ripped apart by a burst of auto-plasma fire.

Normality reasserted itself as Jonelle struggled to her feet and helped her bodyguard get up. "Come on," she said, throwing a glance at Ari, "work to do. Come on—"

Another sound was added to the screaming of the aliens: a bizarre roar. "What the—" Jonelle said, and turned.

From inside the grounded Harvester Ari had hit on first diving through, the one that some of her people had started fighting their way into, a god-awful banging and kicking began. The sound of things crashing, being knocked around—Jonelle looked concerned. "Hey, Team Five," she said down her commlink, trying to sound matter-of-fact after having an Ethereal in her brain, "don't mess up the hardware, we can *sell* that—"

From inside the Harvester, bizarrely, came laughter. "Not us, Boss!" someone shouted. And someone else added, "Won't be much left in here worth salvaging after these guys are through with it!"

And *cows* burst out: three of them. They looked awful—more like demon cows from some confused hell, with bones showing through their coats, with tubes sticking out of them, and wounded sides where they had been gouged for tissue samples. They were fiery-eyed, bellowing creatures, wild with abuse and rage, and now wild with liberty. Jonelle was suddenly irrationally glad that all the Chryssalids seemed to be dead. *I don't think I could handle a Zombie cow at this point.*

A small crowd of Sectoids burst from behind some alien maintenance equipment, firing heavy plasmas and flinging grenades at the X-COM personnel. They ignored the bellowing, rampaging cows. This was possibly a mistake, as the first cow out of the Harvester, a brown one that Jonelle suspected was Ueli's Rosselana, threw up her head and bellowed defiance, then plunged at the Sectoids and gored the Sectoid leader, lifting him on her horns and tossing him some twenty feet away onto a grenade that one of his own people had thrown. This promptly exploded and blew the Sectoid to bits, the timing producing such a slapstick effect that a lot of the X-COM assault troops who saw it burst out laughing helplessly.

Jonelle laughed too. "Come on," she shouted down her command frequency, "let's get 'em!"

With their own versions of her laughter, all of which became more terrible as the rest of the hour went by, the troops followed Jonelle, and whether the aliens fought them, or fled, mostly they died. Furious at the sight of their dead comrades as they passed the ones already fallen, or as more fell, the X-COM people went on, fighting in cold and bitter rage, until they had gone as far down into the alien base as strategic needs required. The whine of weapons and the sporadic lightning of their fire racketed inside the mountain for a long time, and the sweet burnt smell got stronger all the time.

Then, at the end of the hour, Jonelle sounded the recall signal.

Taking everything of value with them—alien equipment, lab materials, Elerium, weapons, captured aliens, corpses, and, with some care, the furious and belligerent cows, who had to be stunned first—the X-COM troops retired to the transport ships, which came in the smoking entry and opened up for them. Jonelle wanted her people out of there before there was time for retaliation, in more strength, to come from space. She refused to leave until the last ship, the Avenger, was ready to go, and Ari, the second-to-last one out, pulled her in.

They lifted out and away. "How did we do?" Jonelle said, still gasping. It was reaction now, and she didn't mind.

Dispatch, which had been keeping score, said down her commlink, *"We lost two Interceptors, one Lightning, and a Skyranger. They lost six Scouts of various kinds, two Harvesters,* two Terror Ships, and an Abductor. Everything that was inside at the time. We have twelve dead. They have—no count yet. Still compiling, but better than a hundred and twenty, I'd say."

Jonelle nodded, getting her breath. "I'll talk to you when we get back," she said to Dispatch. "Out."

The commlink cut. Jonelle reached behind her and swung the cockpit door shut. Then she said to Ari, absolutely furious now that she had leisure to be, "Now I want you to tell me *whatever* made you pull that goddamned crazy stunt! I swear to God, you're going on charges this time. There is no way in hell I'm going to be able to justify this to the Powers That Be. They *saw* our timings four days ago, they *know* exactly what was planned, they are *not* going to believe anything I tell them about us having discussed this previously—we never did—or about me telling you to do any such dumb-ass thing, because they'll have the comms recordings! If you have to do crap like this, why don't you do it in ways where your fellow beings, deluded besotted creatures that they are, can cover *up* for you afterwards? Now I'm going to have to—"

"Explain to Command how, because I hit that Harvester, I saved an entire alien research facility from getting away and being damaged or destroyed. Complete with the research materials, still alive...those cows. Who saved a few people's lives," Ari added, "besides that business with the grenade. Have you seen those girls *kick*?"

Jonelle looked at Ari and finally made an expression of extreme resignation. "I'm going to take this out of your hide later," she said.

"Promises," said Ari with relish, "promises. Damn," he added as the com squawked, "looks like we've got something coming in."

Jonelle looked through the cockpit windshield, and her heart clenched inside her. Coming over the mountain, straight at them, was an alien Battleship.

"Three times lucky," Ari said. Intent on his controls, even while the terrible huge thing began firing at them, he zigzagged, then slapped the controls and let one last fusion ball loose. It streaked away, and Ari cut his thrust and dropped the Avenger straight down about three hundred feet. There were screams of surprise and outrage, and sounds of things crashing into other things from the troop compartment, as everyone went briefly weightless, then got their weight back again as Ari accelerated once more, about two and a half Gs worth, hard off to the right of the Battleship.

The fusion ball hit it amidships punching a gaping hole into its side. Pieces rained down out of the fireball and onto Scopi, and alien bodies fell down out of the black cloud of the explosion, gently and slowly, like snow, into the snow. The great craft hovered, then headed straight for the horizon at a slower than normal speed.

Jonelle gulped. "Dispatch," she said. "Add one damaged Battleship to the count. Are all our craft out of the way?"

"Yes, ma'am."

"Good. Track that ship out, then call for the cleanup."

They headed for Andermatt—and behind them, through the dawn, abrupt and blinding, fire fell from the sky.

* * *

Within hours, all the major news agencies in the world were carrying the story of how a Boeing 797 airliner, belonging to a freight carrier carrying a cargo of explosive materials to Southeast Asia for use by a gold-mining cartel, and a United Nations cargo plane, carrying "humanitarian supplies," suffered a catastrophic collision over the Swiss Alps and crashed onto Mount Scopi, narrowly missing the hydroelectric plant nearby and destroying some of the upper part of the mountain. No local people were killed, but the force of the crash and explosion had been so tremendous, and the terrain was so remote and inaccessible, that it was feared that the bodies of the crew would never be found. Their names were given to the press, and the story made all the major papers. People went "tsk, tsk" on five continents, and then forgot all about it. Nothing remained of the disaster but scraps of twisted metal, which soon rusted or were buried in the snow and ground down into the body of the glacier, which—as it had been for centuries—was slowly twisting its way down the north side of Scopi. Already snow and ice were compacting down into the crater formed by the explosion, sealing it. Scopi's peak was simply a slightly different shape these days, and no one particularly cared.

The X-COM assault force came back to Andermatt and started dealing with the inevitable: healing the human wounded, burying the dead, processing the alien wounded and captured, stacking the corpses, and assessing and storing the consumables and the items that needed to be processed, catalogued, or sold. Jonelle knew she didn't need to supervise this, but she did, for a while, until the weariness began to catch up with her. Then she went to her office to call DeLonghi.

Except for one minor local raid, it had been quiet at Irhil and its catchment area today—but Jonelle was unwilling to bet that condition would last. "I'm sending your complement back to you," she said, "minus a couple. My apologies, Joe."

He sighed. "The fortunes of war. Congratulations, Commander."

"Hold the triumph, Commander," Jonelle said. "I'll be down in the morning, after I get a good night's sleep. I want to have a nice long talk with Trenchard."

He sounded slightly surprised. "I'm sorry, Commander, I thought you'd heard about that. He's gone."

"*What?*"

"As you ordered," said DeLonghi, "a team went to secure him as the operation was about to get under way. But he was gone. I had the place searched, but he couldn't be found, and no one even saw him leave, or had any idea where he might have gone." DeLonghi paused. "Now that I think of it, though—that little local raid we had—"

"An hour or two after he went missing, was it?"

"As a matter of fact, yes. It was a Scout. We lost its trace, briefly—then picked it up again."

"But the Scout itself got away."

"Yes. At the time, with the major operation going down, we needed that Interceptor back here. I recalled it when it was plain it had lost what it was chasing."

"Damn," Jonelle said softly. "Well, you did right. As for Trenchard, damn it, I should have had him put on ice earlier. This one's my own fault—you can be *too* secret, I guess. Well, there's no point in crying over spilt milk. But have the civil authorities in Irhil look for him anyway. If there's the slightest chance that he missed his ride...."

So it was that police forces all over the planet were alerted to look for Jim Trenchard. They looked in vain: no sign of him ever turned up. Jonelle had his quarters carefully searched for any clue or suggestion as to where he might have gone, what he might have intended. She found nothing. The research in his computer was all wiped. Most of his research associates' files had been wiped as well, by hidden "Trojan Horse" programs he had apparently put in place in their computers long before. After a couple of weeks, she gave up, closed his file, and forwarded it and all his materials to X-COM Central for them to deal with. But she could not quite get out of her mind one scrap of paper that had been pinned up on Trenchard's office wall, among his niece's crayon drawings and the Far Side cartoons. It said, in his neat, small print, IT IS BETTER TO REIGN IN HELL THAN TO SERVE IN HEAVEN.

If he was where she thought he was, then by Jonelle's definition of such things, he was in hell, all right. Often, as time passed, Jonelle would wake up in the middle of the night and wonder whether, among the aliens, there was now a human becoming increasingly more Ethereal, another master of that cold hand that had closed around her heart—perhaps a far deadlier one, able to control humans more effectively with fear because it understood those fears so much better. Or, an equal possibility, perhaps they now had among them an Ethereal who remained annoyingly human and threatened to make *them* more so. Jonelle still wondered what Trenchard might have told them, or might now be telling them, that would endanger Earth further, selling out his own people for the bizarre ideal of some impossible and inhuman future that might never need to happen. *Never mind that*, she thought. *If I ever run across him, orders or no orders, he'll be "shot while trying to escape."*

Meantime, there was nothing she could do about it. "Uh oh," Joe said down the phone just then. "Got an interception."

"Go do your job, Commander," Jonelle said, weary. "I'm going to get a meal, and some sleep."

In Andermatt the next day there was a small parade through the town's main street—of several weak, scarred, tired, sick-looking cows, which nonetheless wore the satisfied expressions of creatures who were having a big fuss made over them. Ueli's brown Rosselana was there, and a thin, weary-looking black pugniera called Portia, the one that had been taken from Münster, the town the aliens had raided twice (apparently because they missed the genetically valuable pugniera the first time), and another one called Dutscha, a spotty cow with a foul temper. With her UN hat on, Jonelle had only been able to say to Ueli, when he asked for explanations, "Apparently the aliens think your cows are special." She was not able to explain anything about their recovery, just that they had been "found in the mountains," which was true enough.

A day's stay in Irhil M'goun, where Ngadge and his people had checked them over, revealed little except that the cows' immune systems seemed unusually robust. "That alone would be useful to the aliens," Ngadge said. "We've theorized for a long time that the reason they keep stealing cattle is because they have trouble breeding them." The day's stay had also resulted in one of the lab modules being kicked nearly to pieces—the cows did not like *anyone* who looked like someone carrying lab equipment, a fact that suggested how unpleasant their stay with the aliens had been. But they had survived, which few of their kind had before, and now they swaggered down the street in Andermatt. Ueli, following them, stopped with Jonelle by the door of her little office.

"Well," he said, "it's not too late to start thinking about the next betting season...."

"Oh, Ueli, look at them," she said as Ari came up to join them. "Give them a break!"

He shook his head and smiled. "The way 'they' give you one?" he said. "You look terrible. Circles under your eyes."

"It's the filing," Jonelle said, with a glance at Ari. She was beginning to have her suspicions about what Ueli knew about goings-on in the locality. "Takes it out of you something shocking."

"Come have a drink," Ueli said, "and don't tell me all about it."

They went to the bar, and ahead of them the cowbells bonged softly. Up at the top of town, church bells answered. At the sound of them, Jonelle smiled, considering that, for the moment anyway, she could relax: the demons were held at bay.

Until tomorrow....

Other Proteus Books

The 7th Guest: A Novel
Matthew J. Costello and Craig Shaw Gardner

For the more than one million enthusiasts who have made The 7th Guest one of the best-selling multimedia computer games of all time, this is a must-have book. Here, at last, readers will learn the complete and true history of the mad toymaker, Henry Stauf. Here, too, readers will learn the full story of each of the seven guests and why they were drawn to Stauf's mansion to spend a night of terror.

Game-scripter Matthew J. Costello and his collaborator, Craig Shaw Gardner, open up the story of *The 7th Guest: A Novel* in new and unexpected ways. Whether the reader is familiar with the game or not, this novelization of *The 7th Guest: A Novel* will provide a truly frightening experience. For fans of *The Haunting of Hill House* and *The Shining,* this atmospheric haunted-house novel is the perfect bedside companion . . . but don't turn out the light!

Matthew J. Costello, who wrote the game script fo
The 7th Guest and its sequel, The 11th Hour, is currentl
collaborating with a popular horror novelist on anothe
multimedia game. Costello is also the author of The Tim
Warrior novels, *Time of the Fox* and *Hour of the Scorpior*
as well the *Seaquest DSV* novelization, *Fire Below,* and th
novels *Home* and *Darkborn.* He is a contributing editor t
Games Magazine and writes for *Sports Illustrated, Writer*
Digest, and *Amazing Stories.* He lives in Ossining, Nev
York, with his wife and three children.

Craig Shaw Gardner is the author of many novels, ir
cluding *The Other Sinbad,* which is part of The Sinba
Series, in addition to the novels in The Ebenezum Trilog
and The Cineverse Cycle. He also wrote the movie nove
izations of *Batman* and *Batman Returns.* He lives just ou
side of Boston, Massachusetts.

The Pandora Directive: A Novel

Aaron Conners

"I was picturing a Star Trek kind of crowd, people wh
are interested in lighter science fiction . . .

—Aaron Conners, on designing the gam

Enter the mean streets of Old San Francisco in the yea
2042. Under a Killing Moon is the third and best-know
in a series of popular computer games based on the futu
istic adventures of hapless private eye Tex Murph
Project Bluebook was the official government investiga

tion of Unidentified Flying Objects that investigated, among other things, the "incident" at Roswell, New Mexico. The official story has been told: The Roswell crash was a balloon, nothing more. Project Bluebook was closed. But the real story is that Project Bluebook became Project Blueprint. How does Tex come into the story? Well, he meets an old man in a bar who's looking for his friend who's been missing. It doesn't seem like much of a case at first, but then Tex Murphy has never been very good at staying out of trouble . . .

Aaron Conners is uniquely qualified to write the premier novel based on Under a Killing Moon because he co-created the game with Chris Jones. Conners admits to losing a weekend every year re-reading The Lord of the Rings from beginning to end. He lives in Salt Lake City, Utah.

Hell: A Cyberpunk Thriller—A Novel
Chet Williamson

A hundred years in the future, the most popular game machine ever invented, the ActiDeck, has been outlawed. Plugging directly into the brain, the machine was found, too late, to cause widespread birth defects in its users. Now personal ownership of all virtual reality devices is forbidden. Into this world, the gates of Hell have opened, and the Hand of God party controls the government of the Holy Protectorate of the United States.

Celebrated horror novelist Chet Williamson weaves a tale of terror and intrigue in which two lovers, Gideon

Ashanti and Rachel Braque, run for their lives to escape the fatal consequences of a visit to their home by a government "scrub team." Gideon and Rachel must thread their way between zealous government theocrats and treacherous demons from the underworld in a world gone insane. Readers will learn the answer to the ultimate mystery: How did Hell come to Earth, and who is behind it all?

Chet Williamson is the author of more than half a dozen novels, including *Ash Wednesday, Reign, Mordenheim,* from TSR, and *Second Chance.* His shorter work, nominated for awards, has appeared in *Playboy, The New Yorker,* and *Esquire.* Williamson lives in Elizabethtown, Pennsylvania.

Wizardry: The League of the Crimson Crescent—A Novel

James Reagen

More than 5 million Wizardry games have been sold worldwide since the first game debuted in 1981, and they have already inspired a series of popular novels in Japan. Now the first English-language novel to be based on Wizardry has been written. Novelist James Reagen brings readers an exciting original novel set in the Wizardry universe—where anything can happen! Bill is just an ordinary guy living an ordinary life, until he walks into a cave on a camping trip and finds a sword that gives him extraordinary powers. In no time he finds himself locked in battle against a race of cat people and becomes the only hope for a race of down-trodden human slaves. Before

long, Bill meets a faerie union organizer, has a run-in
with a professional boxer who happens to be covered
with green scales, and gets mixed up with a motley
bunch of revolutionaries who call themselves . . . The
League of the Crimson Crescent!

James Reagen is the managing editor of *The Ogdensburg
Journal.* He lives in Ogendensburg, New York.

Star Crusader: A Novel
Bruce Balfour

One of the most compelling and critically acclaimed science fiction games comes vividly to life in the novel adaptation of Star Crusader by Bruce Balfour.

Star Crusader is the thinking person's science fiction
game, and Balfour has created a novel that will appeal not
only to the hardcore science fiction fan, but also to an audience that demands a compelling plot in a high-tech setting.

Protagonist Roman Alexandria must battle his own
conscience as wing leader for a starfighter force in the
Gorene Empire, as the Gorene crusaders sweep through
the galaxy, imposing their will and way of life on each
civilization they contact. Much like the perpetrators of
earth's own bloody Crusades, the Gorenes are ruthless yet
secure in their moral superiority. Roman Alexandria and a
handful of others have doubts, however, and those
doubts turn to bold action as their commander, the
Gorene General Ferrand, intensifies his relentless assault
on defenseless worlds.

Balfour has created a galactic vision unique and yet disturbingly familiar—and guaranteed to attract a wide variety of readers.

Bruce Balfour is an accomplished game designer in addition to being a successful short story writer and the author of Prima's *Outpost: The Official Strategy Guide*. In a former life, Balfour was employed by the Space Sciences Division of NASA's Ames Research Center to research artificial intelligence applications for interplanetary exploration. This is his first novel.

From Prussia with Love: Castle Falkenstein—A Novel
John DeChancie

"Castle Falkenstein is a breath of fresh air in role-playing . . ."
—*Pyramid Magazine*

"It's full of originality, learning and real wit . . ."—*Valkyrie*

"If you have not picked up a copy of Castle Falkenstein, go and do it right now . . . Highly recommended."—*Capital City*

In the tradition of Gibson and Sterling's *The Difference Engine* and Tim Powers' *The Anubis Gate* comes a steampunk epic! In this magical alternate history of the late 19th century, King Ludwig of Bavaria rules a mad empire of lords, ladies, spies, and scientists in a world where dragons, dwarves, and advanced steam technology are the norm. When Ludwig's secret agents discover that his arch enemy, General Bismark, is developing a steam-powered intracontinental ballistic missile, something must be done! Enter Tom Olam, a man of the 20th century who's been thrown back in time, who agrees to lead a team of spies for Ludwig. Their mission: infiltrate and sabotage Bismark's missile program. Meanwhile, Ludwig launches his own program, using an Italian fireworks expert, to create a solid-fuel ballistic missile. The pace reaches the level of a Tom Clancy novel and never lets up!

John DeChancie is the author of numerous popular fantasy novels that remain perennially in print! His works include The Kruton Interface series, *Bride of the Castle*, *Castle Dreams*, *Castle Spellbound*, and co-authorship of *Dr. Dimension: Masters of Spacetime*.

Other Proteus Books
Now Available from Prima!

Celtic Tales: Balor of the Evil Eye—A Novel $5.99
Nadine Crenshaw

In The 1st Degree: A Novel $19.95
Dominic Stone

Hell: A Cyberpunk Thriller—A Novel $5.99
Chet Williamson

The Pandora Directive: A Tex Murphy Novel $5.99
Aaron Conners

From Prussia with Love: A Castle Falkenstein Novel $5.99
John DeChancie

The 7th Guest: A Novel
Matthew J. Costello and Craig Gardner $21.95

Star Crusader—A Novel $5.99
Bruce Balfour

Wizardry:
The League of the Crimson Crescent—A Novel $5.99
James Reagan

To Order Books

Please send me the following items:

Quantity	Title	Unit Price	Total
_____	_____	$_____	$_____
_____	_____	$_____	$_____
_____	_____	$_____	$_____
_____	_____	$_____	$_____
_____	_____	$_____	$_____
_____	_____	$_____	$_____

Subtotal	$_____
7.25% Sales Tax (CA Only)	$_____
8.25% Sales Tax (TN Only)	$_____
5.0% Sales tax (MD only)	$_____
7.0% G. S. T. Canadian Orders	$_____
Shipping and Handling*	$_____
Total Order	$_____

*$4.00 shipping and handling charge for the first book and $1.00 for each additional book.

By telephone: With MC or Visa, call (916) 632-4400 Mon.–Fri., 9–4 PST.

By mail: Just fill out the information below and send with your remittance to:

Prima Publishing
P.O. Box 1260BK
Rocklin, CA 95667

Satisfaction unconditionally guaranteed

Name_____

Street_____ Apt._____

City_____ State_____ Zip_____

MC/Visa #_____ Exp. _____

Signature_____

About the Author

Diane Duane is the author of several Star Trek novels including the *New York Times* bestseller *The Wounded Sky*. She also wrote two fantasy series, "The Door" series for adults and "The Wizardry" series for young adults. She lives in Ireland.